Son of the Lamp

To Jenny,

with best wishes

[signature]

Charles Eades is a young author who has been writing short stories since he was eight years old. He lives in Macclesfield in Cheshire. *Son of the Lamp* is his first published novel.

Son of the Lamp

Charles Eades

Son of the Lamp

Olympia Publishers
London

www.olympiapublishers.com
OLYMPIA PAPERBACK EDITION

A CIP catalogue record for this title is
available from the British Library.

ISBN: 978-1-84897-126-4

This is a work of fiction.
Names, characters, places and incidents originate from the writer's
imagination. Any resemblance to actual persons, living or dead, is purely
coincidental.

First Published in 2010

Olympia Publishers
60 Cannon Street
London
EC4N 6NP

Printed in Great Britain

Dedication

Florrie Fox 1930-2009

Robin Eades 1934-2004

Two much loved grandparents

Acknowledgments

My parents, brother and sister and other assorted relatives, numerous friends, my teachers, in particular Robin Chambers who first encouraged me to get published.

Prologue

The young man and Loki peered out from behind the ledge.

'She's inside,' said the young man. He got up and ran into the road, Loki following. It was late afternoon, the winter sun low in the sky. Their two shadows, already very long, stretched out behind them as they darted past the rows of houses. It was quiet; there was no-one else in sight.

They reached the house and stopped outside the gate. Both were young, practically boys still, neither of them older than fifteen. Loki was the taller, handsome and dark-haired with a mischievous glint in his eye. His companion was fair-haired and slightly thinner, with less developed features.

'Why are we doing this?' demanded Loki.

'I'll explain later,' replied his companion.

'You keep saying that.'

'This is neither the time nor place for lengthy explanations!'

'Fine, then let's get this over with.' They pushed open the gate and walked quickly up to the front door. 'Are you going to knock or shall I?' asked Loki.

'I'll knock,' said his companion. He knocked once,

twice, three times. They waited for a moment or two. The door opened.

Genie Academy

The first thing Chris knew was that he was lying down. He felt comfortable, so he concluded he was in bed. He was not sure if he had been dreaming, nor did he know how long he had been asleep. As the last remnants of sleep left him, he opened his eyes.

He was in a bed, with white sheets, a white pillow and a white quilt. In fact, looking around, he saw that everything around him was white, from the paint on the walls to the floor to the other beds on either side of him. The room was long, bright and cosy-looking, and the bed was really quite nice and warm. For a moment, Chris was tempted to go back to sleep, but as he blearily attempted to take stock of his situation, he realised he didn't have a clue where he was, and he couldn't remember how he got there. With a growing sense of bewilderment, he discovered he couldn't even remember who he was or where he came from in the first place. He sat up and stared around him.

He desperately tried to think what he had been doing before he fell asleep, where he had been and how long ago, but there was nothing. The room was completely unfamiliar, everything around him was unfamiliar. Even his own body felt like a stranger to him.

At last, he couldn't take it anymore.

'What the hell is going on?' he screamed.

This brought a young woman in a white coat running. 'Is anything the matter?' she asked in a motherly sort of voice.

'Where am I? *Who* am I? And what am I doing here?' demanded Chris all at once.

'Calm down dear, I think it's just the trauma. I suggest you lie down and you'll feel better after a rest,' replied the nurse gently.

'Hold on, I think my name is Chris. Chris… Forrester. Am I right?'

'I expect so. Now lie down and you might remember more later.'

'But…'

'Perhaps this will help…'

The last thing Chris remembered was the woman's eyes staring deep into his own and then everything went black.

When Chris woke up for the second time, the nurse was gone, but there was a man standing at the end of his bed. He looked to be in his forties, with brown hair just beginning to go grey at the edges and a kindly face that was smiling across the bed at Chris now. The smile stayed on the man's face as he spoke: 'Ah, good to see you awake, old fellow. And how are you feeling?'

'Am I still here? Where am I?' demanded Chris, suddenly remembering what had happened earlier. 'Calm down,' said the visitor soothingly. 'Your name's Chris, isn't it?'

'I think so.'

'Well then, I'd better explain. Some parts will be hard for you to believe I'm afraid, but just bear with me and everything will be fine. Now, in answer to your first question, you're in the hospital wing.'

'Of what?'

'All in good time. Now, what do you remember?'

'Waking up here. And then there was a nurse…'

'Ah yes, Nurse Tulip. Then?'

'She stared at me and I fell asleep. I think she hypnotised me or something…'

'Yes, that is one advantage of having magic powers.'

Chris' eyes widened. '*What* powers?'

The visitor looked flustered. 'Oh dear, I fear I may have revealed a little too much already. I'm not sure you're well enough to know everything yet.' But Chris wasn't giving up. 'I feel okay, apart from a slight headache and overwhelming confusion!' he assured the man.

The visitor nodded. 'Naturally. Can you stand?' Chris got out of bed, still a little shaky but his feet managed to support him and he was able to walk over to where the man was standing.

'Hey, I'm still wearing my clothes,' he exclaimed, noticing his jeans, trainers and black jacket for the first time. 'Hold on, how do I remember wearing these?'

'No idea. The human memory is a funny thing.'

17

answered the man. 'Now, come along.'

He led Chris out of the white room into a corridor, which led them through a tunnel to a pair of doors marked MAIN CORRIDOR. Opening them, the man beckoned Chris forward to a sight that made him gasp. A huge hall lay before him, stretching in all directions. A massive staircase led up to another floor, while dotted around the hall were several doorways leading to different corridors. In the centre of the hall was a marvellous fountain, where a golden man looking like a character from "The Arabian Nights", complete with turban and flying carpet, stood with a lamp in his hand. Water spurted from the lamp's spout to add to the liquid splashing at the statue's feet.

'What is this place?' asked Chris in wonder.

'This, my boy, is the Genie Academy,' answered Chris' companion.

'*Genie* Academy?' repeated Chris.

'I'm afraid so. I suppose you know what a genie is from the stories of the "Arabian Nights". It's a spirit that is trapped inside a sealed object, like a lamp or a bottle. If released, he or she must grant three wishes to the person that has let them out.'

He gazed at Chris sadly.

'Chris, it is my duty to inform you that henceforth you are, in fact, a genie. Don't ask how it happened because we don't know. All we know is that someone particularly powerful has trapped you in some object in the mortal world and whilst your soul has been confined in that manner, your body has been sent here.' He paused, to let

Chris grasp the enormity of what he was being told, then continued.

'But if someone releases you from your miniature prison, you have to grant them three wishes using magic. This is a school where we train genies to use their magic as is required by whoever may gain their services. It's not just children that come here. There are quite a few adults, most of whom go on to become teachers, like me. I'm your head teacher, Mr Djinn.'

Chris at this point was still trying to get his head round what had happened to him, so he didn't bother asking whether Djinn was his real name. 'So let me get this straight,' he said hesitantly. 'I'm a genie?'

'Yes,' answered Djinn.

'You're a genie?'

'Correct.'

'This is a school for genies?'

'Affirmative.'

'And I can do magic?'

'Absolutely! Here, let me demonstrate the sort of thing genies can do.'

Without further ado Mr Djinn flew up in the air, circled the hall several times and landed gracefully back down beside Chris. Chris looked at the other people in the hall to see if they were staring in wonder as he was. A couple of them applauded, but most of them took no notice, as if they saw that kind of thing every day.

'I'm going to learn to do that?' said Chris in wonder.

'And lots of other things besides,' replied Mr Djinn,

smiling. 'Come on, we need to get you signed in.' He led Chris to an office with a door labelled: SCHOOL SECRETARY.

A lady of Asian appearance sat in a chair typing at the keyboard of a very large computer screen. She wore a simple secretary-like jumper and long skirt that almost reached her high-heeled shoes.

'Chris, this is our secretary, Miss Sato,' said Djinn.

'Pleased to meet you, Chris,' said Miss Sato, looking round at them.

'Miss Sato, could you inform Chris where he'll be staying during his time here?'

Miss Sato typed at her keyboard and then looked back at Chris. 'I think it best if you stay in room 29. You'll be sharing with Joe Edgar, who happened to be our most recent arrival until you came. I'll call him here.' She pressed a button on the intercom and said: 'Would Joe Edgar please report to reception. Thank you.' Almost the moment she finished a scruffy boy of Chris' age appeared in a puff of smoke in front of them.

'Ah, Mr Edgar,' greeted Djinn, unfazed. 'This is Chris. He's new, just arrived today. I wonder if you wouldn't mind sharing your bedroom with him.'

'Sure,' answered Joe. Then he leaned towards Chris. 'I can teach you how to appear and disappear like that if you want. It's brilliant! I use it to get to every lesson!'

'Joe, what have I told you about misusing magic?' said Mr Djinn sternly.

'Sorry,' muttered Joe.

'And now perhaps you could take Chris to your room. Chris, here's your timetable.'

He handed Chris a sheet of paper. 'You'll start lessons tomorrow; for today you can adjust to your new surroundings. I trust you'll be comfortable.'

Joe led Chris to the room they'd be sharing. It was fairly simple, with two beds at either end of the room and a few posters of famous genies. Miraculously, Chris' bed had already got his name on the end. He collapsed on it in a daze. 'So, what lessons you got tomorrow?' asked Joe. Chris looked at his timetable.

'Period two, I have Performing Magic with Mr Djinn. But period one is Surviving Magic with Miss Torment.'

'Same lessons as me, then. Performing Magic's great, although Mr Djinn does sometimes get carried away with his demonstrations. As for Surviving Magic…you'll get used to it.'

'So how long have you been here?'

Joe frowned and counted the days on his fingers. 'A year I think, although it's hard to tell in this place. Time passes slowly. You know some of the pupils here have been in this school for decades and they look about twelve!'

'And how did you get here?'

'Can't remember.'

Chris smiled faintly. 'That's funny. Neither can I.'

'No-one can. It's weird; for some reason no-one that comes here can remember who turned them into a genie, who they were before it happened or where they came from. At least it's better than missing all the people you've left behind.'

Chris shook his head. 'Not really. I'd prefer to miss someone rather than not remember who's missing me back in the mortal world. Where is this school anyway?'

'Come and look out here,' Joe led Chris to the window. Chris' mouth dropped open. What he thought had been mountains in the distance were actually clouds, stretching off into the horizon. Night beginning to fall, and the stars shone like diamonds in a great expanse of darkness above them.

'Are we above the earth?' asked Chris, his voice almost a whisper.

'Mr Djinn reckons we're in some sort of netherworld, outside time and space. We still have night and day, but they're sort of artificial,' explained Joe.

Chris frowned. 'So if we're genies, does that mean people rub our lamps, or whatever they are, and let us out?'

Joe nodded, and then seemed to change his mind. 'Sometimes. But it doesn't happen often because whoever turned us into genies must have really hated us and wouldn't particularly want us to get out. You remember Aladdin's cave? Well, that's probably the sort of place they're likely to have left us.'

Chris asked the question that was most on his mind. 'So how do we get out? How do we become human again?'

'Someone wishes us free. It does happen. But it would

have to be a very kind owner to do that. Most would want all three wishes instead of one reserved. When you're a genie, it's a painful reminder of how greedy people are.'

Chris sighed. 'Well, if we're stuck here together for the next few millennia, what are we going to do to keep ourselves occupied?'

Joe grinned. 'Just you wait and see!'

First day

The next day, Chris was woken by the amplified voice of Mr Djinn echoing through the school: 'WAKE UP EVERYBODY! TIME FOR ANOTHER EXCITING AND ADVENTUROUS DAY OF POSITIVE LEARNING! BREAKFAST IS AT 8.00! PLEASE DON'T STAY IN YOUR ROOMS PAST THAT TIME, OR THE BED BUGS WILL EAT YOU!'

'Bed bugs?' repeated Chris sleepily.

'He means it,' replied Joe. 'At 8.05 all the tiny insects that lurk in the bedrooms grow to enormous sizes. They don't make any mess; they just root around looking for dead skin. Unfortunately, if you're still here when they grow, they have trouble distinguishing between dead skin and live skin, so you might want to hurry up.'

Chris did hurry; in fact, he was out of the room barely five minutes later so he and Joe were among the first in the dining room. Breakfast was whatever they asked the dinner ladies to conjure up. Interestingly, Chris managed to remember that his favourite cereal was cornflakes, though he was too groggy to realise at the time. At 9.00, lessons began.

Surviving Magic, it turned out, was simply PE involving magic. But it was obvious from the start that

Miss Torment didn't treat it at all like PE, with or without magic. She was a broad, muscular woman wearing combat gear and with all the tough, snappy nature of an army sergeant.

'Now listen up punks!' she barked at Chris, Joe and the other twenty assembled boys and girls as they stood in the large, cold sports hall. 'I hear we have a new member today. This is Chris. Hello, how are you, nice weather we're having, introduction over, shut up! Boy next to Chris?'

'Yes miss?' answered Joe nervously.

'Show new kid how to change into lesson uniform! As for the rest of you, in your own time!'

Chris watched in amazement as all his classmates changed into combat gear in a puff of smoke. Joe turned to him. 'It's quite simple really. Just picture yourself wearing the same clothes as us and count to three.' Sure enough, Joe's clothes appeared on him as he was speaking.

Taking a deep breath, Chris closed his eyes, counted to three and then opened them. He didn't feel any different, but when he looked down, he discovered he was wearing brand new clothes in the same style as everyone else.

'That's enough chit-chat, eyes to the front!' yelled Miss Torment. 'We're starting a new topic today! Gymnastics!'

The class groaned.

'Oh stop complaining! I expect you'll find it easier than troll wrestling, and God forbid you do any worse on this than you did on that! For the next four weeks, you punks will learn how to dodge fireballs blazing at you from all directions, how to fly through lightning storms without being electrocuted, and how to play *extreme* basketball! And believe me; you're all going to get A stars if it kills you! If it weren't for the fact you're genies, it probably would!'

One hour later, Chris, Joe and the rest of the class trailed into Mr Djinn's classroom, exhausted and, in most cases, slightly singed. Chris could remember certain details about gymnastics as it was in the mortal world, and it definitely wasn't nearly as *exhilarating* as the way Miss Torment taught it. Chris certainly couldn't remember running across the hall with the teacher hurling fireballs at him back home. He had done surprisingly well; Miss Torment had commented on his speed when he had finished; but that was before she raised the stakes and began hurling lightning as well. One boy had made the mistake of trying to fly through the magic barrage, and had been blasted out of a window. Torment had been right: it was very lucky they were immortal genies with automatic healing powers.

The entire class collapsed in their chairs as Mr Djinn greeted them with an enthusiastic grin. 'And how are we today?' he asked cheerfully.

'We've just had Surviving Magic, sir,' replied Joe. He hadn't been as fast as Chris.

'Oh, I see. Miss Torment's been having fun with you has she?' Djinn's question was answered with dour looks from the class. 'Cheer up. Today we'll be doing more on granting wishes. Now who can tell me the golden rule of wish granting? Yes Amelia?'

The girl next to Joe lowered her hand and said: 'Genies can grant any wish except the Forbidden Wishes.'

'And the Forbidden Wishes are?'

'Killing, Love and Resurrection.' answered the girl.

'Quite right. The Forbidden Wishes are the three things a genie cannot grant its master or mistress. It's not a matter of principle; we physically can't grant them. A genie cannot kill anyone, they can't make someone fall in love with someone else, and they can't bring a deceased person back from the dead.'

Chris cautiously raised his hand.

'Yes, Mr Forrester?' said Mr Djinn.

'I'm guessing genies aren't the only wish granting magic creatures in existence sir?'

'Oh, certainly not. There are also fairies, leprechauns…' The teacher thought for a moment. 'Mind you, leprechauns tend to lie about granting wishes when they're in sticky situations.'

'But can they grant the Forbidden Wishes?' persisted Chris.

'Fairies can.'

'Doesn't that make them more powerful than genies?'

Mr Djinn's mood turned sombre. 'There's something you need to understand about fairies, Chris. As a race, fairies are generally alright. You get the occasional black sheep but that's the same with every species. No, it's the fairy godparents you have to watch out for; after all, they're the ones who grant wishes. You see they're not like the fairy godparents in children's tales. There are no pumpkin carriages, white mice or bippety-boppety-boos to be seen; the real thing is slightly less friendly. Fairies can be summoned by the parents of a child and instructed to watch over and protect the infant. But the fairy doesn't just watch over its godchild; it owns them. There may be no limits to what the fairy can grant their godchild, but it doesn't *have* to grant them wishes like we do.'

His gaze swept the classroom, and his next remarks were clearly aimed at them all.

'There are reasons why the Forbidden Wishes are impossible for genies. A mortal human can kill someone with his bare hands; he doesn't need magic to help. Give someone the power to kill with the click of a finger and who knows what corruption it might cause. As for love, that's the most powerful emotion in a person's head. A fairy can grant it, but they can't get it right. They'll just make someone think they're in love, and that'll cause more pain for both parties.

'And bringing people back from the dead would be a disaster! Even fairies seem afraid to try it because all previous attempts have resulted in ghosts, poltergeists and sometimes even zombies. So yes, fairies are more powerful wish-granters than genies, but for completely the wrong reasons. And yes, there are some things a fairy can do that I wish I could do. Like refuse to grant a wish.'

'What would happen if a genie refused to grant a wish?' asked Joe.

'I don't know,' answered Mr Djinn. 'But I wouldn't like to find out.'

The next lesson Chris and Joe had was History of Magic with Mr Abdullah. The classroom they entered looked like the interior of a tent, with lots of decorations that seemed to have come from the Middle East, including Mr Abdullah himself. He wore a turban, a cloth shirt that exposed his chest, dark brown trousers and a huge scimitar slung in a scabbard on his belt.

'Salaam, my young class!' he greeted them.

'Salaam, Mr Abdullah,' droned the class in unison.

'Have a seat!' The class all sat down on mats laid out on the floor. 'Now then! Today, you'll be learning about the rise and fall of the Elf Empire and the rise of the fairies!' At that moment Mr Abdullah gave a fierce cry, drew his sword and embedded it in the floor a few centimetres from the face of a terrified-looking boy next to Chris.

'I will not have chewing gum in my class!' shrieked the teacher. 'Spit it out!'

'I can't sir,' said the quivering pupil.

'Why not, insolent dog!'

'I swallowed it.'

Abdullah glared at the boy. 'Do it again, and I'll turn you into a camel!' He picked up the sword, sheathed it and went back to the front of the classroom. 'As I was saying,' he went on as if nothing had happened.

'For many thousands of years the most powerful race in the mortal world was the elves! A fine and noble race whose empire spanned much of the earth. Strictly speaking, it wasn't an empire, more like a collection of kingdoms of different elves. But in times of trouble these kingdoms would rally together against the enemy, the fairy race! There were many wars between the elves and the fairies. The main reason for this bitter rivalry was because they were so similar; in appearance, in their level of magic, in their intelligence. But the elves had something the fairies didn't have. A weapon. A secret weapon of incredible power, the likes of which mere genie fools cannot fathom!'

Abdullah walked over to the blackboard and drew his sword. 'For millennia the elves used it to remain the most powerful race. But then, as suddenly as it appeared, this weapon disappeared.

'No-one knows what happened to it. Some say the elves hid it; some say it was destroyed by fairy spies. But whatever the reason, the elves lost their only advantage over the fairies and within a few hundred years their empire had collapsed. For the next couple of millennia the fairies were the dominant race; but it was during this time that a new power came into the world: Man.'

Using his sword as a pointer, Abdullah conjured up a picture on the board of a person, with *all* the body parts showing and labelled.

'Despite their complete lack of magic, they had intelligence and the ability to build.

And as the humans forged their civilisations across the face of the world, the magical species were forced into hiding. Now there is increasing tension between the elves and the fairies, as whatever land unclaimed by humans is squabbled over by the other races. The rainforests, the sea, even Antarctica are areas with boundaries disputed by elves and fairies alike.'

'Do you think there'll be another war sir?' asked Joe.

'Maybe,' replied Abdullah. 'The thing is, if there is another, this time I fear it will be much bigger than the previous ones. Because over time the fairies and elves have forged alliances with other magical races. If another war starts, this time it may involve the whole world.'

'Even the genies?' asked Chris.

'Put it this way, an army of genies, even without the ability to kill, would be an unpredictable weapon. We can only hope that at this point in time no-one knows this netherworld exists, but if someone should find a way to come here and take it over, Allah help us all. Hey! Are you chewing again you son of a jackal!'

That night, as he lay in bed looking out at the cloudscape bathed in moonlight, Chris thought over the day's events. He still couldn't quite believe what was going on. It was as if he'd suddenly been born into a completely different universe. There was a whole world out there of magic and mayhem that he had yet to experience. Too bad he was stuck here in Genie Academy. But that was okay, there'd be plenty of excitement and new things to learn here.

Even if he never returned to the mortal world, Chris

had no doubt he was going to enjoy the years ahead immensely. He just wished he could remember what he had left behind in the mortal world. Presumably he would have family out there, friends and relatives who would be worrying about him. Could he really enjoy himself that much if at the back of his mind there was the knowledge that someone in the mortal world was missing him? Still dwelling on these thoughts, he slowly drifted off to sleep.

The sun illuminated the darkened alley. Chris watched the figure running. Another figure stood behind them, arms raised. A flash of light. The running person fell. Insane laughter.

A voice.

'Loki?'

'Yes Chris?'

'I need your help.'

Chris was woken a few hours later by a cry. Looking across the room, he saw Joe tossing violently in his bed and occasionally crying out. Cautiously, Chris got out of bed and crept to Joe's bedside. As the screams became more frequent and louder, Chris took his friend by the shoulders and shook him roughly. Joe woke with a cry and thrashed about until he saw Chris standing beside him.

'You alright?' asked Chris.

'Yeah, yeah I'm fine. Just…just a bad dream that's all,' replied Joe, panting heavily.

'Are you sure?'

'I'm fine! Just a dream. Go back to sleep.' Joe turned away and lay down again. Chris returned to his own bed, but watched Joe carefully. He saw the other boy take something from around his neck. It was a necklace, with a locket on the end. Joe opened the locket and gazed at something inside. Then he noticed Chris watching and put it back round his neck before lying back. After a while Chris heard him snoring gently.

'Loki...' he whispered, his voice almost lost in the night.

Soon he was asleep too.

Lessons in the art of magic

A few days later, Chris and Joe had another Surviving Magic lesson with Miss Torment. 'Okay, punks!' she barked at the class. 'Today you're going to learn how to play *extreme* basketball!' She summoned an ordinary-looking basketball out of thin air. 'The rules are simple. You will be divided into two teams and will attempt to levitate the ball through the opposing team's hoop without it touching the floor. And believe me; you really don't want it to touch the floor. If it does, this ball will explode in your face! Don't cheat, or you will die. Don't handle the ball with your hands, or you will die. And don't let it fall to the floor, or everyone in the vicinity will die! And remember, it's not the winning that counts, in the end it's just the survival of the fittest!'

Later on, Chris came to understand this principle, because if it weren't for their immortal powers, there would have been several casualties in that one lesson. First of all, Miss Torment divided them into the teams and summoned basketball nets to each end of the gym. Then she threw the basketball up in the air and blew her whistle to signal the start of the game.

What followed was complete and utter mayhem. Each player had to keep the basket ball levitating in the air, and with both teams levitating in competition with each other, the ball would frequently hit the floor and explode, throwing debris and pupils everywhere, or else it would crash into a wall and cause more destruction. Many times Chris, Joe and the others were thrown off their feet and after less than twenty minutes Chris was bruised and scorched all over -as were the rest of the class - with the score at nil-nil.

Outside the gym, Mr Djinn and Miss Sato were walking together through the corridor when they heard the noise. 'Sounds like they're playing extreme basketball again,' remarked Miss Sato.

'Yes, I think they're having fun, don't you?' said Mr Djinn.

He was interrupted as an explosion disintegrated the wall next to them and they were both thrown to the floor. Mr Djinn got up angrily and used his own powers to levitate the ball up and throw it back at the pupils. He watched as it exploded against the far wall and, satisfied, helped Miss Sato up as the wall behind them mended itself by magic.

Back inside the gymnasium the pupils continued to be battered by numerous explosions as the ball was thrown all over the place, along with shards of wall and ceiling. The only person who seemed to be enjoying herself was Miss Torment, who watched the pandemonium with glee safe inside her protective shield. That was until Chris found the ball headed straight for him and wildly shot a levitation blast at it. The ball went sailing through the air so fast it crashed through Miss Torment's shield and she disappeared in a flash of fire. The whole class looked at Chris with a mixture of admiration and horror. Chris himself looked more than slightly terrified. The smoke cleared and Miss Torment stepped out, her clothes smouldering and her face blackened, but what showed of it was a picture of utter fury.

'Down on your knees and give me one thousand press-ups, Forrester!' she snarled. 'And report to detention this afternoon!'

Chris didn't hesitate in doing as she said. As he laboured away Miss Torment barked at the rest of the class: 'And the rest of you aren't going anywhere until he's finished! And should anyone of you miserable little punks ever do that again, it'll be two thousand press-ups and a one-way ticket to your own private hell, is that understood?!!'

'Yes miss.' said the frightened mutterings from those of the pupils who had the courage to speak.

'Good! Now get on with it, Forrester!'

Later that day, Chris and Joe had Magic Art with Madame Le Louet. She was French, as her name suggested, and dressed in a glamorous black dress with tons of makeup and eyeliner on her face.

'Today, *la classe*, I shall teach you the wondrous art of painting by magic.' She droned in her mournful tones. 'It is a method of painting that goes back almost to the time this academy began! There are those who possess the gift of the magic artist, and those who do not, but remember anyone can be an artist if they put their mind to it! Because that is what Magic Art is all about. The mind!'

The class were all seated in front of sheets of paper mounted on easels with paintbrushes in their hands. 'Er, miss?' said Chris.

'*Oui*?'

'We don't have any paint to paint with.'

'My darling, a true magic artist does not require oils and colours to paint a picture! Just clear your minds and the picture will paint itself. Whatever you see in your mind's eye will be preserved on the paper forever! Now hurry up, s'il vous plait it is nearly time for le déjeuner, and that should never be delayed.'

Chris attempted to do as she said, but found he couldn't keep his mind focused on one image for long enough. It didn't help that he was still exhausted from his ordeal at the hands of Miss Torment. She hadn't let him go until he had completed all one thousand press-ups and though Chris had more strength in him than most boys his age thanks to his magic, the exercise had still taken a great deal out of him both physically and mentally.

'Remember, true relaxation and concentration is the key.' Madame Le Louet droned on. 'You must not let your mind wander. You must be clear about what you are painting otherwise the canvas will not be able to create it. But be careful; if you concentrate too hard the painting may come alive.'

This warning was given a trifle too late, as no sooner had the teacher finished speaking than Georgina

Armitage's painting of a gremlin, leapt from the canvas and started charging around the classroom trashing easels and making a mess. As the gremlin continued to make a nuisance of itself a knight in shining armour stepped out of Frank Marner's picture. 'Fear not peasants; I shall slay the beast!' cried the knight, drawing a huge sword from his scabbard and running after the gremlin, which dodged and stuck its tongue out at him as it led him in a chase through the classroom and out of the door. In the stunned silence that followed Madame Le Louet turned to the class with an expression of "I told you so" apparent on her face. 'Continue with your work,' was all she said.

The distraction did nothing for Chris' concentration, and by the time the Magic Art lesson was over, all he had to show for his efforts was something that vaguely resembled a mutant monkey eating Mr Abdullah while being chopped to pieces with an axe by Miss Torment. Chris looked over at Joe, and was surprised to see Joe sitting before a perfect portrait of a girl their age that Chris didn't recognise. 'Who's that?' he asked.

Joe looked at him strangely, then he took the locket from around his neck and gave it to Chris. Chris opened it and saw a photograph of the girl in the picture.

'I don't know who she is,' explained Joe, sadly. 'The locket was around my neck when I first arrived here. I think I might have known her before I came.'

'Maybe one day you'll be released, and you'll get to see her again.'

'Maybe,' replied Joe, though he didn't sound hopeful.

He turned to the portrait and pointed at it, and it burst into flames.

That afternoon Chris went with a deep sense of apprehension to his detention. He was relieved to find out that Miss Torment would not be overseeing the detention; instead he would be spending it in the library. The first thing that Chris noticed about the library was that it was huge. Shelves of books stretched away into the distance and the enormous walls lined with books old and new seemed to go up forever.

'I take it you're the new boy.'

Chris spun round in surprise. An elderly, hunch-backed man was watching him through scrutinising eyes.

'Yes,' answered Chris, feeling uncomfortable under the old man's gaze.

'I don't believe we've met,' said the old man. 'I'm the Librarian.' He turned away as if that was all he had to say.

'And what do I call you?' asked Chris.

'Just the Librarian,' replied the Librarian. 'Now, I believe you were sent here to serve a detention. You can start by making yourself useful and dusting the shelves. *Without* magic.'

The Librarian tossed Chris a duster and he immediately set to work. After half an hour he had come to realise that cleaning without magic really was a suitable punishment; the dust of what seemed like a hundred years had accumulated on the bookshelves and there were so many that Chris was making slow progress. As he worked the Librarian sat at a desk nearby reading an old tome.

'How many books are there in this place?' asked Chris.

'Who knows?' replied the Librarian. 'And don't ask how we acquired them. If you come in here looking for a particular book it'll be here, never mind what kind. It's as if the library just knows what books are needed and always has them ready. I've been here five hundred years and it's always been the same.'

Chris looked up in surprise. 'Five hundred years?' he repeated. The Librarian nodded grimly. 'According to the school records, I've been here the longest. I used to have a lot of friends here. But, one by one, they've all been released. Only I remain. You don't age here.' he said, sighing. 'You just get tired, and it shows. Look at the young head-master. Only been here twelve years and already he's going grey. Just goes to show, doesn't it? Now, carry on with your work. There's a lot of dust still here.'

The next day, Chris was walking to lunch on his own when he came to a corridor he hadn't been down before. It led into a circular room with a very high ceiling. Coming out of the corridor, Chris saw the walls were adorned with pictures of people, men and women alike. Some were young, some old, some smiling, and some frowning. With a start Chris realised he wasn't alone. Mr Djinn was standing gazing at one photograph of a smiling middle-aged man. He turned and noticed Chris standing there.

'All the previous head teachers of the Genie Academy.' said Mr Djinn. 'Most of them at least. Bearing in mind genies only worked out how to create photographs using Magic Art a couple of centuries after this place was founded.'

'Who's that?' asked Chris, pointing at the picture Mr Djinn was standing in front of.

'My predecessor, Mr Link,' answered Djinn, sadly. 'He was headmaster when I first arrived here, taught me everything I know.'

'What happened to him?'

'Five years after I came he was summoned to the mortal world. The diamond in which he was imprisoned was discovered by a witch who let him out. Everything went downhill for him after that. The witch who owned him was particularly cruel; she used her wishes to make him do horrible things. Then, when all three wishes were granted, she used her own magic to release him.' His face became even grimmer. 'I think that was the worst thing she did to him.'

'Why?' asked Chris.

'When a genie is released they get their memory back, but Mr Link had been here so long that all his friends and family were long dead. When he became aware of this, it broke his heart. He used the diamond to regain his powers and became a genie again, then returned here a broken man. Nurse Tulip and the other medical genies did their best to look after him, but I think he'd lost the will to live by then.'

'What happened?'

Mr Djinn sighed to himself. 'He committed suicide. He

destroyed the diamond that had been his prison. It's the only way to kill a genie. That's what put me in charge. You may wonder why, considering there are people who have been here much longer than me. Well frankly, I don't think anyone else wanted the job.'

'Why's that?'

'Because every head teacher Genie Academy has had has ended up dead. That's quite an achievement for a genie. And every time one of our genies goes to the mortal world, the whole thing seems to end in tragedy. Sometimes I wonder if it's better that we stay in this place, because when I think of Mr Link and other old friends I've lost through their being summoned, I wonder how long I'll last as headmaster.'

Mr Djinn fell silent, then he laid a small rose underneath the picture of Mr Link.

As the weeks went by, Chris discovered that he was really quite good at magic. Not only was he a fast learner but he could maintain certain spells for longer than most of his classmates. From Mr Djinn he learned how to summon things out of thin air, and how to throw fire, lightning and other elemental weapons; and Joe kept his promise to show Chris how to appear and disappear at will and then how to fly.

Growing in confidence, Chris got an A star on his Performing Magic coursework, levitating objects; his flying carpet became a popular source of transport among his classmates. As much as he detested Surviving Magic, he was getting pretty good at it. Despite her gruff army nature, Miss Torment was a good teacher who recognised talent when she saw it, mainly as a target for her fireballs. Chris knew he would soon need this talent, because the gymnastics examination was drawing near, and no-one could be truly sure what sort of unbelievable fright fest Miss Torment would decide to cook up.

One day Chris' class had a joint lesson with Miss Torment and Mr Djinn. They took the class outside the school grounds, where they walked amongst the cloud surface of the netherworld. There the two teachers showed them how to manipulate wind and use it against their opponents. Once he had got the hang of it, Chris was able to blow Joe off his feet and use the wind to carry himself into the air, and he could even create small tornadoes that blew and whirled all across the grounds. Soon the whole class were having a great time.

From a distance, Mr Djinn and Miss Torment watched the pupils practicing.

'Makes you smile, doesn't it?' commented Mr Djinn. 'When you see them having such fun with magic. It takes your mind off the harsh reality of being a genie.'

'In my experience, John, that harsh reality is what defines us,' replied Miss Torment.

'But it gives me hope,' continued Mr Djinn. 'Hope that they won't be doomed to stay here for the rest of time. I mean they're young, they don't deserve that. They all have lives to go back to, not like old fogeys such as you and me. Trying to help them escape this netherworld is what keeps me going.'

'It's not getting them out of here that worries me,' said Miss Torment. 'I see it as my duty to train them for the trials posed by the magical world. If they can't withstand my lessons then they won't survive out there. I learnt a long time ago that the magical world is a far nastier place than the mortal one. If any of those young people over there leave this school they'll need guts to keep going when they reach the world that awaits them.'

'I understand what you're saying, Nadia. But I believe there is hope for them. And besides, even if none of them leave here, we must still make sure they are fit to train those yet to arrive. As Alan Bennett once said, "Pass it on".'

'Who's Alan Bennett?'

The Pit Of Doom

A few days later, at the end of the last Surviving Magic lesson before the exam, while the class were getting back on their feet after a particularly fierce extreme basketball game in which the exploding ball had been twice as powerful, Miss Torment beckoned them to her.

'Okay punks!' she snapped. 'We won't see each other until next Wednesday, which is the day of your gymnastics exam. Now remember, you may think you're doomed, and you probably are, but remember we genies stick together!'

'Oh great,' muttered Joe. 'It's her "into the fray" speech again.'

'Though we are but flesh, and blood, and bone, and muscle, and nerves, and hair, and hormones, and anything else that exists in our bodies, remember punks, we are a great family of genies who stand shoulder to shoulder as we charge into the fray! Though our bodies may be broken, our limbs severed, our brains spattered over the ground as our organs are ripped from our lifeless corpses; we fight as one, and die as one! At least we would if we were mortal. So my message is, punks, make me proud! Now get out!'

'With pleasure,' said Joe quietly as he, Chris and the

rest of the class trailed out.

On the morning of the examination, Miss Torment led the class out of the building and across the grounds.

'Right punks!' she barked. 'Today's your gymnastics examination! The task I've set you will require everything I've taught you this month! Agility, persistence, imagination, and above all, the will to live! You will need all of these to survive the journey across the pit of doom!'

The teacher pointed to the bottomless pit they were heading for. Fire erupted from its bowels, and huge tentacles reached up to grab any unsuspecting prey. High above the tentacles, a thin rickety ladder ran straight across.

'This particular pit of doom just happens to be home to the caretaker's pet fire kraken!' explained Miss Torment. 'And she hasn't been fed today. Your task is to climb across the pit on that ladder bridge without falling off. If you fall, well, be thankful you're immortal. You'll be going in alphabetical order. First up: Josh Atkinson!'

Josh took a deep breath and scrambled up the ladder. He almost made it. Halfway across, his hand slipped and he plunged in. His use of flight saved him from falling into the tentacles of the fire kraken but he was still scorched by flame. Gloria Bentley was less lucky. She was doing well until one of the tentacles reached up, grabbed her and threw her into the distance. Miss Torment clicked her fingers and the girl reappeared in a heap in front of them.

What followed was ten minutes of agony for Chris as one by one his classmates' names were read out and each one went to meet their fate. None managed to reach the other side and several were carried away on stretchers. Joe Edgar was immediately before Chris and would have succeeded if a jet of flame hadn't chosen that particular moment to shoot up and blast him off the ladder. He reappeared on a stretcher, scorched black and belching smoke. As the nurses carried him away, Chris waited apprehensively for his name to be read out.

'Chris Forrester.'

Chris sighed as if his death sentence had been announced, and walked reluctantly towards the ladder.

Grasping the cold metal, he began to climb. Slowly and carefully he made his way up, not daring to look down. Every minute he expected to hear the hiss of flame rushing up to meet him or see the tentacle coming ever closer.

But, as he reached the top, he realised they weren't his only worries. The ladder bridge was still badly scorched where it had been engulfed by flame. It didn't look strong, and Chris was unsure whether to go really slowly or really fast. In the end he chose fast and scrambled forward, hardly daring to breathe, praying that the bridge would hold.

It didn't.

The whole thing gave way and the section immediately behind him broke off.

Clinging to that portion of the ladder which still hung from its moorings on the other side, Chris watched the broken section fall into the fiery abyss. 'Okay. Don't panic,' he muttered to himself calmly. 'All you need to do is switch to flight and you'll be across in no time.' Only then did he notice the tentacle reaching up for him.

'Oh drat.'

The tentacle wrapped itself around his body and pulled him from the ladder. Thinking quickly, Chris closed his eyes and within a second he erupted in flames. Every patch of skin on his body was now on fire, and the smell of burning flesh came from the tentacle.

The kraken released him with a rumble that sounded like thunder, but could have been a deep groan of pain; however, Chris wasn't concentrating on that. Still burning like a torch, he swooped through the air across the pit, dodging tentacles swinging at him from all directions. One collided with him and sent him spinning straight over the remaining section of ladder at the far edge.

He landed with a thud, rolling across the ground until he came to rest at the feet of Miss Torment, who had just materialised on that side of the pit. Chris got up shakily, no longer burning, but still slightly blackened.

'Am I still alive?' he gasped.

'Just about. You get a B. Next time try and make it a better landing. Oh, and well done,' replied teacher, with the ghost of a smile.

Chris beamed and turned towards his cheering classmates all of whom were heading his way. Suddenly, he felt like he could face anything anytime and come out on top.

Which was just as well.

His euphoria about the Surviving Magic assessment was cut short the next day by a completely unexpected occurrence. It was during the morning break, as Chris went to meet Joe outside that he was stopped by Mr Djinn in the main hall. 'Morning Mr Forrester,' said the headmaster. 'I heard some good things about you from Miss Torment, and that's quite an achievement in itself. She said you were the only person in your class to make it across the pit of doom.'

'Uh, that's right, yes,' replied Chris, blushing slightly.

'Don't be embarrassed about it; you're a very powerful genie. I don't know what it is that makes some genies more powerful than others, but it might be something to do with our lives as mortals.'

A sad look entered Mr Djinn's eyes. 'It's a great tragedy that none of us can ever remember what happened before we came here. I haven't been here very long, but even those that came before me have no recollections of who they used to be.'

'How long have you been here?'

'I think about thirteen years. That might seem a long time but teachers like Miss Torment have been here for centuries, maybe whole millennia.'

Chris found it hard to imagine being at the school for a thousand years. The thought prompted his next question.

'How long has this school been running?'

'There's nothing in the records about when the Genie Academy was founded, but I think the school has been standing since the first magicians walked the earth.'

Mr Djinn smiled at him, but his eyes were still sad.

'There are many magic users in the mortal world, some of whom were around long before the humans. You get witches and wizards, but the main magic users are the non-human ones that live in dark places humans will probably never set foot in. Some are mainly bad, some are mainly good, and some are simply victims of another creature's evil, like us genies.'

His eyes had a faraway look. 'One day, I hope, everyone in this academy will be freed, instead of the occasional one every few years. And if...' Mr Djinn paused. '*When* that day comes, I hope you and I are around to see it.'

Just then, Joe saw them and headed their way.

'Ah, here's your friend Mr Edgar,' said Mr Djinn. 'I'll apologise for keeping you.'

But just as Joe reached them, a strange feeling came over Chris.

His whole body tingled, and he felt as if something were pulling him somewhere; but whatever it was had no idea which direction it should take him in, and so was tugging at him from all sides.

Chris looked down, and to his horror, saw his entire body was glowing. Lightning crackled around his feet and magic fire circled him. He looked up at Mr Djinn, Joe, and the sudden crowd of students who had noticed what was going on and come running.

'What's happening to me?' he asked, addressing everyone in general.

'Oh my God,' exclaimed Joe in wonder. 'You're being summoned.'

'Summoned?' repeated Chris.

'He means your lamp – or whatever – is being rubbed,' explained Mr Djinn. 'Your new master or mistress is summoning you.'

'Come on everyone!' cried Joe. 'Let's give him a decent send-off!'

With that the whole crowd started clapping and there were a few shouts of 'Good luck!'

'But wait!' protested Chris. 'I'm not ready! I've only been here a month! So many spells to learn! And where are my shiny shoes? I need my shiny shoes! I want to go to the mortal world in my shiny shoes!' The last thing Chris saw of the Genie Academy was Mr Djinn's smiling face, and then he disappeared in a flash of light.

The Summons

'Chris?'
A voice on the edge of blackness.
'Look at me, Chris.'
So weak. Difficult to focus.
'Chris, it's Loki.'

Chris came to. He hadn't expected to be summoned so soon after arriving at Genie Academy. From what Joe had said, he hadn't expected *ever* to be summoned. And if he *were* ever to be summoned, he had pictured himself materialising in a puff of smoke wherever he had been summoned to. He hadn't pictured himself rocketing down a tunnel of flashing colours at the speed of light. 'However, at the time the only thought in his head was: 'AAAAAAAAAAAAAAAAAAAAAAAAAAAAAAAA AAHHHHHHHHH...!'

After a length of time impossible to measure, Chris could see a circle of white light rapidly growing in size at the end of the nightmarish tunnel. If he had been in an entirely different frame of mind, he might have considered the possibility that he was, in fact, dead. But his brain was still too focused on the 'AAAAAHHH!!!' to think about this. The light came ever closer, until it enveloped him; there was a brief moment of sheer whiteness, then the feeling of being peremptorily ejected from something.

Without so much as a 'Look out!' to warn him, Chris found himself in a small attic room, flying through the air in the precise direction of a heavy-looking bookshelf. He had barely a second to register this fact before he crashed into it. Chris allowed himself to fall onto the floor, books raining all around him. 'That wasn't so bad,' he muttered to himself.

Then the bookshelf itself toppled over, crunching into several parts of his body with a sickening crack. After the quick healing of a number of broken bones, Chris summoned the energy to lift the shelf and push it back against the wall. The books flew into their former positions on its shelves, and the cracks in the plaster disappeared as if by magic.

Slowly, Chris got up, groaning slightly from the stiffness in his body, and stood with his back against the wall. It was only then that he realised he wasn't alone.

A girl stood opposite him. She wasn't much younger than he was, maybe thirteen or fourteen, and Chris noticed that she was quite pretty; he could tell she was going to be very beautiful when she was older. Her hair was strawberry blonde, and her eyes bright blue. Despite her surprised expression, she had the face of someone who often gets what they want. Not conceited; *stubborn* was nearer the mark. Chris found himself wondering if she'd been in any fights at school, because despite her good looks she gave the impression of being rather fierce. Then he looked down, and saw what she was holding.

It was a lamp. *The* lamp. The one he had been imprisoned in all this time. And Chris realised with a shock that this girl was his mistress. The lamp itself was just like the ones used in "Arabian Nights", old and dusty and a dull yellow in colour. Chris felt a little privileged that he had been sealed in the classic genie prison. But then his mind came back to the person who held it. He hadn't really had time to wonder who his owner would be, but he could tell now he hadn't wanted one of the opposite sex. This was going to complicate matters slightly.

'Um, hi,' he said, his mind a blank on the subject of opening conversational gambits.

'Who are you?' demanded the girl.

Chris drew in a deep breath. There was nothing for it but the truth.

'Well, I'm afraid this is going to be a bit hard to explain. Better start with the basics. I am a genie. You are my mistress. Happy now?'

'No.'

'Didn't think you would be. Okay, let's start over. I'm the genie of that lamp you're holding, and given the fact that you've just rubbed it and let me out, you're my mistress and I have to grant you three wishes. Are you with me so far?'

The girl didn't look convinced. 'You're a genie?'

'Yep.' He grinned. 'I can tell this is going to be just like my first day at Genie Academy but the other way around.'

The girl folded her arms. 'Prove you're a genie.'

Stubborn was definitely the right word.

'Well considering I just flew out of that lamp in a spectacular and very painful manner – an entrance that would have made Robin Williams applaud - do you really need any more proof?'

Yes, she did. 'How do I know you're not some burglar that got his hands on some fancy lights and fake smoke?'

Chris always welcomed any opportunity to show off his magic.

'Fair point. Okay, can a burglar do this?' Chris turned himself into a lion. 'Call me Simba!' he said out of the lion's mouth. 'Can a burglar do *this*?' He became human again, but instead of there being just one of him he began to multiply, each clone shouting 'Duplicate! Duplicate! Duplicate!' until there were ten of him standing in a row.

'Can a burglar do *this*?' they asked in unison, before becoming one again and bursting into flames. 'Look at me, I'm the Human Torch!' yelled the flaming pillar. 'Except I'm not American, and a good thing too!' Chris laughed maniacally. He had a good maniacal laugh. It had come in handy during school plays when he was mortal. Hold on, how did he remember that?

'Alright, alright!' interrupted the girl. 'You've proved your point.'

'Just as I was starting to enjoy myself,' muttered the fiery Chris, before the flames vanished. 'So come on then, what do you wish for mis... Do I *have* to call you mistress? What's your name?'

'Lucy,' answered the girl.

'Lucy.' He tried it out and found he liked it. 'Nice name. And I'm Chris, so you don't have to call me genie. Anyway, you've got three wishes. Any three wishes - well, apart from three specific ones but we won't go into that. And no wishing for more wishes please. So what do you want?'

Lucy shook her head. 'Nothing.'

'I'm sorry?'

'Well, I don't need a genie. I was just looking around in here when I found this lamp, and it was all dusty so I rubbed it and you popped out.'

Chris stared at her in bewilderment. 'Okay, but… *three wishes*!'

'Why do I want three wishes?'

'So is this what you're saying? I'm having a nice time at Genie Academy in the clouds, I don't ask to be summoned, I have an unpleasant trip into the mortal world, and when I get here the person responsible doesn't even want my services! Talk about ungrateful! Listen!' He marched up to her and prodded her in the shoulder.

'I'm offering you any three wishes! No payment, no loopholes, no contracts with small dodgy writing and even smaller small print! Just any three wishes. So get wishing!'

'Fine,' agreed Lucy unenthusiastically.

'Great. So what do you wish for? Still no clues? Wish for anything! Wish for… wish for a milkshake.'

'Okay, I wish for a milkshake.'

'What kind?'

'Chocolate.'

'Chocolate! Okay, make it official!'

'I wish for a chocolate milkshake.'

'What's the magic word?'

Lucy sighed in annoyance. 'Please!'

'Great! One chocolate milkshake coming up!' An apron and chef's hat appeared on Chris and a work surface materialised before him. 'This is Chef Jamie Oliver showing you how to make a delicious and healthy milkshake!'

Chris took a blender and started throwing various ingredients in. 'You can use chocolate, ice cream, chocolate ice cream, full milk, semi-skimmed milk, goat's milk, or even, you guessed it, a fire extinguisher!'

(Chris had learnt magic cookery in a lesson with Mr Djinn. Explains a lot, doesn't it?)

Chris turned on the blender. 'Just mix it together and then you have your very own chocolate milkshake!'

Then the lid of the blender came off and the mixture spewed all over Chris. He wrestled with the blender for a moment and then tripped over his apron and fell behind the work surface. Once the noise had stopped, his hand reached up from behind the surface holding a glass filled with milkshake. He placed it on the work surface and added a straw. Then the hand disappeared from view and a shower appeared next to the work surface. It gave Chris a quick rinse before leaving whence it came and taking the work surface with it. All that was left was Chris in his normal clothes holding the milkshake.

'Your milkshake, madam.' He gave Lucy the milkshake, concealing an exhausted sigh. Lucy sipped the milkshake through the straw. 'So how is it?' asked Chris.

'I've tasted better,' answered Lucy absently.

'Tasted better?!' Chris snatched the milkshake off her and drank some himself. Then he choked and gagged. When he'd regained his breath he handed it back, saying: 'I see what you mean. Need to work on my magic cookery.'

Just then a shout came from downstairs. 'Lucy! Are you ready yet?'

'That's my mum. I'm going to be late for the school bus,' said Lucy. 'I'm coming!' she called through the open door. But then there came the sound of footsteps on the stairs.

'You'd better hide. She might think you're a burglar like I did,' Lucy said to Chris. 'I'll go in my lamp. Take the lid off will you?' said Chris. Lucy held out the lamp and removed its lid.

'I hope it's easier going in than it was coming OUUUUTTTTTTTT!!!' screamed Chris as his face, followed by his entire body was sucked into the lamp. As his foot disappeared the lamp's lid flew from Lucy's other hand and landed in its place on the lamp. Chris found himself sitting in complete darkness.

'Any way to see out of this thing?' he asked himself. Instantly the inside of the lamp became transparent, and it looked as if he was sitting on empty air just above Lucy's giant hand. She put him down behind her and turned towards the doorway. A woman Chris assumed to be Lucy's mother walked in.

He could see even from his position on the floor that she was tall and extremely beautiful. She had the kind of lovely golden hair that you always saw on princesses in fairy tale books. She even had the right rosy red colour on her lips, and to go with the striking looks she had an exceptionally glamorous style of clothing. Chris started to wish he had this kind of mother, but then remembered he had no recollection of what his mum looked like. Perhaps he had one just like this woman. As he was thinking these thoughts, he began to get the feeling that he knew her from somewhere...

Lucy's mother smiled charmingly at her. 'You're going to be late darling, you should be going. What are you doing up here anyway?' she asked in a mesmerising voice that would have made her a good hypnotist.

'I was bored Yvonne, I just came up to look around. I am ready.' answered Lucy demurely.

'Well you'd better set off then. The bus will be here soon.'

'I'll be down in a minute,' replied Lucy as Yvonne went back out. Then Lucy turned and picked up Chris' lamp. 'You can come with me to school,' she whispered to him. 'Is there any way you can make the lamp smaller?'

'Sure,' answered Chris, amplifying his voice so she could hear him. 'I'll turn it into a key ring, then you can hang it on your school bag.'

Sure enough, the lamp shrunk and a key ring complete

with clip appeared. Lucy carried him down the stairs and to her bedroom, where her school bag lay on a bed. She attached the miniaturised lamp to it and then slung the bag on her back. Chris was bumped around a lot as she carried him downstairs to the door where Yvonne was waiting.

'Looking forward to another day packed with learning?' asked Yvonne.

'Not really. I've got a maths test today,' answered Lucy unhappily.

'Oh never mind. I'm sure you'll be fine, my little genius.' Yvonne wrapped Lucy in a motherly embrace and kissed her on the forehead. 'Now have a good day, I'll see you after school.' She released Lucy and waved as she walked out of the door and down the path.

When they reached the bus stop Chris asked from inside the lamp 'Why do you call your mum Yvonne?'

'Well she's not really my mum,' explained Lucy. 'I'm adopted. She told me when I was eight, and I've called her by her real name ever since. She doesn't mind.'

'Eight was a bit early to tell you that wasn't it?'

'She thought I was strong enough to handle it. It didn't traumatise me or anything.'

'That's your opinion...' muttered Chris.

'Oy! Anyway, I don't mind. Yvonne's a great godmother, she does anything I want. Well, almost anything.'

'She spoils you?'

'I am not spoiled!' snapped Lucy hotly. 'It's none of your business anyway!'

'Okay, okay. Just asking. I'm the guy in the lamp, asking silly questions. Don't mind me.'

'Sorry,' apologised Lucy in a gentler tone.

'Where are we anyway?' Chris asked to change the subject.

'Camden. My school's just a few streets away.'

'London. It figures.'

They stopped talking as the bus arrived, and it gave Chris time to think. If he was turned into a genie by some powerful enemy in his mortal life, why did they leave his lamp in the attic of a house belonging to an ordinary London family?

Yvonne watched her daughter disappear out of sight down the road. Then she turned and went back upstairs to the attic. Something in her gut was telling her that not everything was right...

She searched the attic for something she had put there, and was now missing. It occurred to her that Lucy might have found it, and it would be very bad if this were the case. Yvonne stood up straight. There was no doubt about it, the thing was lost.

'Drat,' she muttered.

Out of the lamp and into the fire

Chris found his tour of Lucy's school quite interesting, if a little disconcerting hanging in mid-air from Lucy's bag. There were no memory triggers, so Chris didn't think he'd been to this school in his mortal life. The experience also taught him a bit more about his new mistress. She was in year eight, though he'd guessed that already, and didn't have many friends. He also discovered she liked drama and history, but was terrible at maths and science. Chris remembered he was quite good at maths and whispered answers to her while she was taking her test in first period.

He was particularly impressed to hear she went to a karate club held by the school and was already a purple belt. Nice, he thought, she might not do any magic but I reckon she would still be pretty handy in a tight spot. Unfortunately, both he and Lucy found out that she would need this skill that lunchtime in a confrontation that was going to have unforeseen consequences.

Second period, Lucy had history. The teacher was a wacky young man called Mr Peters who obviously enjoyed his job, although Chris was slightly worried when he saw that the teacher carried around a toy lightsaber. 'Morning guys!' he greeted the class enthusiastically.

'Morning, Mr Peters,' intoned the class.

'Well, you could have sounded a bit more enthusiastic. Anyway, before I get on with the lesson I've got something rather interesting to tell you. Who here has been to Stonehenge?' Only a couple of pupils raised their hands.

'You're an uncultured bunch aren't you?' remarked the teacher. 'Well, at the weekend I discovered in the newspapers that they're starting excavating there again for the first time in fifty years! What do you think of that?'

'I think you should read today's paper sir,' said a boy next to Lucy.

'Why's that then?'

'The archaeologists they sent there have disappeared.'

'Really?! Wow! Don't suppose you've got a copy of the paper on your person?' The boy who'd spoken took a newspaper out of his bag and handed it to the teacher.

'"Mysterious disappearance of Stonehenge archaeologists."' read Mr Peters. 'Here, pass it around.' As the paper was passed around the class Mr Peters started explaining about Stonehenge.

'It is believed to have been built five thousand years ago, and there are various different theories as to why. Some say it was a religious site, some a burial ground, others that it was built by magical elves to guard their buried treasure! Don't worry, that last one was a joke!'

When the paper reached Lucy, she scanned the picture on the front page. It was of a crowd of people surrounding the Stonehenge circle. Looking closely, she noticed one of the people in the crowd looked a lot like Yvonne. But then she dismissed it as a trick of the light and passed it on.

The next lesson was science with a bloated, frog-faced man called Mr Phobic as the teacher. 'Okay class.' he droned, 'Today we're going to learn about how electricity works. The particles…'

While Mr Phobic put the class to sleep with his excruciatingly boring explanation of how electricity worked, Chris decided he'd had enough of sitting inside his lamp under the table. Turning into a fly, he quietly exited the lamp and flew across the classroom looking for a suitable perch. Then he noticed Mr Phobic had a cage full of budgies on his desk. Thinking that no-one would notice an extra budgie, he flew between the bars and turned into a bird. He looked at the other four budgies.

'Hello, I'm Chris, what's your name?' he said to the nearest one.

'Tweet.' answered the budgie.

'Right. Pleased to meet you too.'

'Tweet.'

Chris turned away from the antisocial budgies and watched Mr Phobic continue to ramble on.

'…and the light bulb becomes a source of heat as well as light.'

Chris was beginning to realise just how much he hated science, and wondered if that had been the case before he became a genie. Whatever the reason, he felt like making something blow up just to liven up the lesson. However, he decided to go for a less dramatic interruption.

'Well, strictly speaking that's not true.' said Chris in a

loud, clear voice. Mr Phobic stopped.

'Alright,' he said, glaring at the class. 'Who said that?'

'Tweet?' said one of the budgies.

Seizing an opportunity, Chris replied 'It was me! The ghost of Lab 3!'

'Whoever that is, stop it before I call a senior member of staff!' threatened Mr Phobic.

'That won't do any good! You'll have to call Ghostbusters to get rid of me!' replied Chris. 'As I was saying, that explanation of electricity is totally wrong! You've been reading too many science books, mate!'

'I'll have you know, whoever you are, that I have a masters' degree in science!'

'Is that so? Well, *I've* got a ghosts' degree in science!'

'And what did that teach you?' This question was a definite mistake.

'That electricity is generated by thousands of tiny little elves all working away to produce light and heat!'

The class began to laugh. Mr Phobic was getting more and more angry.

'Nonsense!' he shouted.

'Who are you calling Nonsense?! The name's Gerald, I'll have you know! And boy, would those elves be insulted if they could hear you now!'

'Stop this right now! I demand you show yourself and stop this silly prank!'

'Or what? You'll throw your O Levels at me?'

By now, the class was laughing hysterically and Mr Phobic had gone puce in the face.

'That's it!' he shouted. 'I'm calling a senior member of staff!' And he marched out of the classroom.

'Tweet.'

Of course, by the time he got back there was no sign of the "ghost of Lab 3" and Chris had returned to his lamp. As a result, for many years after, pupils would claim that Lab 3 was haunted by a particularly rude ghost who liked annoying science teachers and hanging around in the vicinity of budgie cages.

'Tweet.'

At lunchtime, Chris and Lucy had both finished their lunches – which had been prepared using slightly different methods – and were sitting talking together on a bench in the school grounds. Chris was still in his lamp but Lucy had the bag up on the bench beside her.

'Mr Phobic is never going to live that down,' Lucy was saying. 'Just don't do that in any of the other lessons. And as for that maths test, I must have got full marks! I hope the teacher doesn't smell a rat.'

'I'm sure she won't,' replied Chris. 'Although it might have helped if you'd revised a bit more.'

'And I suppose you revise for everything at this genie school of yours?'

'Yes, as a matter of fact. It wasn't all fancy spells; we did have to do written work occasionally. Mind you… Chris was interrupted by a sudden jolt that threw him off balance where he was sitting inside the lamp. It was the jolt of Lucy being thrust violently off the bench, taking the bag with her.

Chris got to his feet muttering something that involved blowing people up when he saw who was responsible.

An enormous girl who stood about a foot taller than Lucy was advancing on her with the smug expression that can only be worn by someone both stupid and cowardly. 'Who you talkin' to, freak?' the big girl demanded with the kind of accent that Chris, with his slightly posh dialect despised. A gang of equally ugly girls, their looks made worse by heavy makeup and designer clothes that were clearly against the school uniform, crowded round their leader staring at Lucy with the same expression.

'No-one,' answered Lucy, staring fiercely back.

'Got an imaginary mate?' continued the older girl, ignoring the previous answer. 'Hey everyone, say hi to the little rat's imaginary mate!'

'Hi, little rat's imaginary mate!' intoned the gang, waving sarcastically in various directions.

'Shut up,' snarled Lucy. In his lamp, Chris was starting to get uneasy. The grin left the other girl's face.

'Shut up?' she repeated, advancing slowly. 'No, I'm not finished yet. I want you to say sorry for tellin' me to shut up.'

'No.'

'No? Well then I'd better teach you some manners.' The girl pushed Lucy so hard that she fell over onto the hard stone ground. The bully stood over her, grinning again.

'Hey look, she's dropped her bag. Let me get it for

you.' She snatched the bag and thrust Lucy back when the younger girl tried to intervene. 'And look!' she crowed, catching sight of the lamp key ring. 'You still watch *Aladdin*? 'Ow sad!' Her chubby hand reached for it.

Inside, as he watched the huge hand coming closer, images came flooding back of the times when Chris had been bullied before he became a genie, before he got his confidence and sarcastic humour. And he got very angry. As the girl's hand closed around the lamp, Chris shouted: 'Is it just me or is it getting *hot* in here?' And he burst into flames. The lamp became red-hot in a microsecond and the bully dropped it with a yelp.

Chris wasn't finished. Flames spat from the lamp's spout onto the girl's trouser leg, and she began screaming and dancing round trying to stamp them out.

'What's going on here?' One of the teachers strode towards them, and the gang scattered, leaving Lucy now standing on her feet watching in amazement and the other girl still desperately stamping on her smoking trousers. The teacher looked from one to the other accusingly. 'She started it!' cried the bully, pointing at Lucy. 'She set fire to me!'

The teacher merely said 'I think you had both better come and see the head.'

Parents were phoned, of course, and that evening after school the bully, who was a year eleven called Agatha Granger, sat with her parents in the head teacher's office facing Lucy, who sat beside Yvonne. The head mistress

Miss Damsel was seated on a chair between the opposing parents. Agatha's mum and dad were fuming, Yvonne merely stared calmly back. Chris was watching events from inside the lamp on Lucy's bag. He had a bad feeling about this meeting. Lucy had assured him earlier that Yvonne would take care of everything, but Chris found that he could not share Lucy's faith in her adoptive mother.

Miss Damsel was equally uneasy. She had had to preside over many discussions with parents regarding bullying and fights in school, which as head teacher she was naturally prepared for. However, she had met Agatha's parents before, and knew them for the stubborn and unpleasant people they were. She had also met Yvonne, and although it was her policy not to make judgements about pupils' parents, since technically she was meant to be working with them to make sure their children got a good education, Miss Damsel had to make an exception for Yvonne. It wasn't that Yvonne was particularly horrible; it was just the way she looked at you as an adult would look at an amusing toddler. Miss Damsel always got the impression she wasn't being taken seriously when she spoke to Yvonne. All Lucy's teachers had similar opinions. However, now Miss Damsel was going to have to supervise this meeting and she wasn't looking forward to it.

'Now then,' she began. 'I think the parents should hear what both students had to say after the incident occurred. Agatha says Lucy threw a key ring full of burning matches at her without provocation, Lucy says Agatha stole her bag, although she can't give an explanation for how Agatha's trousers were set on fire. Now,' she looked from one party to the other. 'Does anyone wish to comment or give a reason for their child's behaviour?'

'Agatha's completely innocent.' announced Mrs Granger. 'She 'as a fantastic record, always does 'omework, and she's the top of 'er class!'

'Top of her class?' repeated Yvonne quietly. 'Fantastic record? I've heard she only comes into school three days out of five, and that her homework is non-existent. Perhaps you're mistaking her for some other daughter.'

''Ow dare you!' cried the other mum, standing up. Her husband took her arm and said 'Calm down, Jo…' But he was cut short by his wife shaking her arm from his grip and using it to point a finger at Yvonne. 'You dare to question my daughter's behaviour? It's not Agatha's fault if her record is ruined by an unprovoked attack by some sneaky, connivin', wicked little daughter of a b…'

'Jo!' interrupted Mr Granger.

'Nor is it Lucy's fault if she is bullied by a girl twice her size with a blind liar for a mother.' replied Yvonne coolly.

'Who you callin' a liar?!!' yelled Agatha's mother.

'If we could all just calm down please…' began Miss Damsel, but her peace-making fell on deaf ears as Mrs Granger continued to shout abuse at Yvonne and Lucy. Chris was getting more and more uneasy. He'd been feeling guilty about getting Lucy into trouble before, but now he was worried he was going to have a fight on his conscience. So he came to a decision.

He transformed himself into the smallest kind of fly he knew about, quietly exited from the lamp and flew unnoticed out of the room and into the corridor. There he took his own shape again and knocked on the door. He only just heard the head mistresses' 'Come in!' over the voice of Agatha's mum. He pushed the door open slowly and poked his head through. The room fell silent. 'Is Lucy in here?' he asked.

'Yes,' answered Miss Damsel somewhat breathlessly. 'But if you don't mind we're in the middle of a meeting.'

'Yes, sorry, that's what I came for,' explained Chris, walking in and shutting the door. 'You see, I saw what happened. Sorry I didn't come forward before, but I didn't know this was going on. Lucy didn't start the fight, Agatha did.'

'What?' demanded Mrs Granger.

'Now Jo, let's hear what he has to say.' said her husband.

'Thank you. Agatha and her gang started on Lucy without provocation, I saw them push her to the floor and grab her bag.'

'And what about the "key ring full of matches"?' asked the head.

'I saw smoke, but somehow I don't think a small key ring could contain matches, burning or otherwise. It strikes me Agatha probably had matches on her person and took them out to set fire to the bag. I expect she dropped a

71

burning one and it set fire to her trousers. Whatever the reason, I'm certain Lucy's innocent. As I was saying…'

'I'm not listenin' to this!' interrupted Agatha's mum. 'This is clearly some jacked-up conspiracy on the part of Lucy an' 'er mother…'

'Shut up, woman! I'm talking!' shouted Chris. This had the desired effect and there was a stunned silence. 'Thank you,' he muttered quietly as if the command had been just as polite. 'As I was saying, Agatha started it and Lucy is entirely blameless. I hope I've been of some help.'

'NO!' yelled Agatha, who had let her mother do the talking up until now. 'You,' she spat, pointing at Chris. 'Are just a lying, tattle-telling little snitch and…'

'I may be a lying, tattle-telling little snitch but *you* are also a liar and a nasty big bully!' replied Chris.

'What…!' began Mrs Granger.

'And you're just as bad,' Chris said to her. 'Only you're also a bad parent because you don't do anything about her behaviour; you just lie and paint a halo around her whenever she gets into trouble, which I'm guessing is quite often!'

The whole room was ablaze now, with everyone joining in the argument save for Lucy, Yvonne and Miss Damsel, the former and latter of whom were looking around in bewilderment, while Yvonne simply stared at Chris as if she were surprised he existed.

'QUIET!!!' bellowed the head at last. Silence fell. 'Young man, I think you've said all you need to say and thank you for coming forward.' she continued. 'And now to the matter still at hand. Mr and Mrs Granger, I appreciate you supporting your daughter so... passionately, but the fact is I think it more likely that Agatha started this affair.'

Agatha's parents immediately began protesting, but were cut off by Miss Damsel.

'She has been involved in bullying incidents many times this year, while Lucy has not had detention once since she arrived. Therefore Agatha will be punished and not Lucy. If you wish to protest further you may, but that is my final decision.'

For once, both Grangers remained silent, though they were both fuming again.

'In that case I think we'll call it a day.' continued the headmistress with barely disguised relief. 'Thank you all for coming, I apologise again for dragging you out here after school. Good night.'

With that, Agatha and her parents exited the office, the women muttering to themselves incoherently. Yvonne and Lucy followed. Chris also left, feeling slightly nervous amongst all these angry parents, some of whom he had made even angrier. He stood outside in the corridor, watching Yvonne and Lucy receding. Then they stopped.

'I'm just going to the toilet.' said Lucy, separating from her mum. Yvonne nodded and watched her depart, before turning her head sharply towards Chris. She raised her hand and beckoned, and Chris found he couldn't stay where he was if he wanted to. He approached her until they were standing face to face (or they would have been had they been the same height. At fifteen Chris was quite tall but Yvonne towered over even him).

'What was your name again?' asked Yvonne, smiling with an expression that looked worryingly like the kind a cat watches a bird with.

'Chris Forrester,' answered Chris.

'Well Master Forrester, I'd like to thank you for what you just did. If it weren't for you, my daughter might have ended up in detention.'

'It was nothing; I just wanted to do the right thing.' replied Chris, shrugging.

'Good for you. Are you a friend of Lucy's?'

'No, I just happen to know who she is.'

'We haven't met before, have we?'

'I don't think so.'

'Have you family of your own?'

Chris was unsure what to say to this. It was a strange question, and the way she kept looking him in the eyes without blinking was beginning to scare him. It was as if she was reading his mind… reading his mind.

Chris began to wonder. Did she know what he was?

'Well, they're nothing interesting.' mumbled Chris.

'Does anyone your age find their parents interesting?'

'I suppose not.'

Chris saw Lucy emerge from the corridor behind Yvonne. Yvonne turned and saw her. Then she smiled at Chris. 'Thanks again. Perhaps we'll see you again sometime. Good night.'

Yvonne joined Lucy, who glared at Chris behind her

mother's back. Chris waited until they were out of sight and then transported himself to Lucy's bedroom.

Waiting there for Lucy and Yvonne to get home, he reflected on the night's events.

He had made friends with several girls back at Genie Academy but what went on inside their heads remained a mystery to him. He couldn't remember much about girls from his former life, so he didn't think he had ever had a close relationship with one.

Perhaps that was why he wasn't doing very well with Lucy. It wasn't that he didn't like her, quite the contrary, she had a fierce and determined personality that he found fascinating, it was just he couldn't understand her. Plus she was younger than him and knew nothing about the magical world save what he had told her. Chris made a mental note to ask Mr Djinn for advice on girls next time he saw him. Heaven knew it wouldn't hurt him.

When Lucy got home, she was not happy. Not happy at all. She had a few reassuring words from Yvonne, a kiss on the cheek, a quick supper and then she went upstairs to change. It was night now, and she was looking forward to a good night's sleep and a blazing row with Chris. One of which she was going to get, the other she definitely wouldn't.

She entered her bedroom, turned the light on and went to the wardrobe. It opened by itself and the amplified voice of Chris announced:

'Hello, and welcome to Lucy's wardrobe. Tonight you'll be wearing pink fluffy pyjamas, a pink fluffy dressing gown, pink fluffy slippers and, you guessed it, pink fluffy underpants!' All these garments were flung at her as their names were read out.

'Thank you for coming to Lucy's wardrobe!' The wardrobe closed itself. Then it opened again. 'Toothbrush,' it added, throwing one out and closing.

'How long have you been in there?' demanded Lucy sternly.

'Twenty minutes.' answered Chris guiltily. 'I got bored. And you have some really interesting clothes in here. Or rather, they're interesting when you've shrunk to a height of ten centimetres and you're stuck inside them. Gets a bit cramped when you're full size.'

'Out!' ordered Lucy. The doors opened again and a full-size Chris stumbled out, dislodging several clothes hanging up. He stood fidgeting slightly under Lucy's glare.

'Well!' he said, trying to brighten up the atmosphere. 'That worked out all right I suppose!'

'Worked out all right?' repeated Lucy. 'Thanks to you I've now got an enemy who's going to give me hell for the rest of the year!'

'After you set fire to her? I doubt it,' replied Chris.

'Agatha won't be scared of me for long. Sooner or later she'll start repercussions.'

'So? You're a karate kid, you can handle yourself.'

'Against an opponent my size, yes. Agatha's nearly twice my size!'

Chris turned away and folded his arms. 'Well it's no

good having a go at me; I've done all I can!'

'No you haven't,' said Lucy.

Chris turned back to her, unfolding his arms uneasily. 'What?'

'You're a genie. You can do whatever I want!'

'Like what?' said Chris suspiciously.

'You could kill her if I asked you to!'

'As a matter of fact I couldn't. Killing is one of the few wishes a genie can't grant!'

'But you could scare her couldn't you? Or make her have an accident?'

'Don't even think about it!'

'Can you?'

'Stop it!'

'Do it!' ordered Lucy.

'No!'

'I'm sorry?'

'I said no!'

'Make Agatha have an unpleasant surprise! I'm not saying I want her injured, maybe just a very narrow escape! Or how about a terrifying visitation in some scary disguise? Come on, I'm the only one getting ideas here, you're the all-powerful slave!'

'I'm not misusing my powers just to help you get revenge on some girl at school! I may be a genie but I have principles!' said Chris angrily.

'I wish for you to go and scare Agatha and threaten to do it again if she doesn't leave me alone!'

'I refuse!'

In that instant the whole world was pain. Chris was in absolute agony. He felt fire enveloping his body, fire and lightning and terrible pain. He collapsed on the floor and writhed, resisting the urge to scream. Lucy just stared down at him in horror.

'What's happening?' she exclaimed.

'I refused to grant a wish!' cried Chris. 'It must be against my magic! Now it's turning on me! It's killing me!'

'Well, grant the wish, maybe that'll stop it!'

'Are you crazy? I might be in agony but I'm not doing that!' he screamed.

Lucy knew what to do. She'd done it only once before and even then she'd been unable to explain how it happened. She just knew somehow that it would work.

Clearing her mind, she placed her hand on Chris' forehead. Chris felt the pain drain away, and the fire that enveloped him withered and died. He could feel her in his mind, harnessing his magic and calming it. Then she breathed out and Chris had control of himself again.

'How did you do that?' he asked bewilderedly, slowly sitting up.

'I don't know,' answered Lucy. 'If I touch someone's forehead, by thinking hard enough I can make their pain go away. I did it by accident once. When the circumstances are right, my mind seems to do it by itself.'

'That wasn't just taking pain away! You took control of my mind and used it to make my magic stop attacking me. I've never heard of such a thing. Still, at least now I know what happens when a genie refuses to grant a wish.'

'Well that won't happen with Yvonne,' said Lucy, getting to her feet.

'What?' replied Chris suspiciously.

'Yvonne can do anything with her magic. She's a fairy.'

Chris' blood suddenly ran cold.

'A fairy? Yvonne's a fairy? Like a fairy godmother?'

'I suppose.' Lucy was acting like this was perfectly normal, while Chris was on the verge of a mixture of panic and pure terror. Then they heard footsteps outside.

'She's coming, get into your lamp!' said Lucy, handing Chris the lamp. Chris disappeared into it and made it fly into a cupboard by Lucy's bed. Yvonne poked her head in the door.

'I heard a noise coming from here. Is everything all right?' she asked.

'Yes, fine,' answered Lucy.

'I suggest you get ready for bed. I'll be up to say goodnight.' With that Yvonne went back out. Lucy whispered into Chris' cupboard. 'If you watch me getting changed I'll kill you.'

'Yes ma'am,' replied Chris' voice.

Later, as Lucy lay in her bed, Yvonne came in quietly, and Chris watched with his special eyesight as she bent over the bed and whispered in Lucy's ear.

'Goodnight. And don't you worry about your friend Agatha; I'll take care of her.'

'Yes, well, don't hurt her. You remember when you

got a bit carried away with that hitch-hiker who pinched your purse,' said Lucy.

'I told you, that was entirely accidental. Anyway, he recovered eventually. I'll simply make sure Agatha doesn't cause you any more trouble. Now sleep,' Yvonne kissed Lucy's cheek, putting a sleeping spell into it that made the girl instantly fall deeply asleep. With that Yvonne straightened up, her face no longer caring. 'And now, Agatha,' she muttered, fire spouting from her hand. 'You'll find out what happens when you annoy a fairy.' Then she closed the hand and left the room.

Chris sat in his lamp feeling helpless. His mind began arguing with itself:

Hold on, I'm a genie, I can stop her!

Yes, but she's a fairy, she's more powerful than me!

So? She can't kill me, I'm immortal!

True, but she could give me a good battering.

Oh, will you stop worrying! I'm going to stop her, and that's that!

Fairy spelled backwards is Trouble

Using her own tricky magic, Yvonne discovered Agatha was in a car on the motorway, probably off to visit a relative – after all, it was Friday. She got into her own car and transported it to the stretch of road, and as she got nearer to the car Agatha was in, she thought over her thirteen year plan. It was a good thirteen year plan, one of the best she'd ever had. At least it was better than her eighteen year plan involving a servant girl and a glass slipper. How was she to know the girl's stepmother had been a fairy as well? It had taken quite a long time for Yvonne to hear the end of that fiasco.

Still, this one was going well, and if it went as well as planned it would make Yvonne the most powerful fairy alive. But what about the boy? She hadn't expected to see him again. Would he cause her trouble? Yvonne made a mental note to make some enquiries about him once Agatha was taken care of.

She had drawn up directly alongside Agatha's car. This was going to be fun. Behind her, an invisible Chris watched from the backseat. Yvonne smiled and spun the steering wheel.

The car rammed into the Grangers' car with such force that Chris was thrown against the window. He reflected that perhaps it would have been a good idea to wear a seatbelt.

Laughing, Yvonne rammed into the neighbouring car again and again, forcing it further across the motorway. Chris realised if she carried on she would cause an accident. Still maintaining his invisibility shield, he flung his arm around Yvonne's shoulders.

She struggled against him fiercely and Chris fought desperately to hold on, having clearly underestimated her strength. He lost control of his invisibility shield and when she was able to see him Yvonne grabbed his arm and swung him over her shoulder. He smashed through the windshield and was forced to cling to the bonnet with a hand that had been transformed into a large magnetic clamp.

'You!' hissed Yvonne, and pointed a finger at him. Fire burst from her hand and Chris gritted his teeth as the heat scorched his skin and set his clothes on fire. Fortunately for him Yvonne could no longer see where she was going because of the flames and careered into the metal fence that separated the two roads. The contact sent the car up into the air, over all the other cars with their drivers watching in amazement and off the motorway into a field nearby. The car went spinning boot-over-bonnet until it came to rest just upright in the middle of the field, windows smashed and steel badly scratched.

Yvonne shook herself in the driver's seat. Her head was bleeding, but it would soon heal. She looked around for Chris. Then she saw him get up from the ground a few yards away. He had fallen off when the car exited the motorway. With a determined expression, Yvonne started the car and drove straight towards him. Chris saw her speeding in his direction and realised he didn't have time to transport anywhere, or do anything.

He closed his eyes and waited for the impact.

It never came. Without realising he was doing it, Chris had cast a spell that turned his body to smoke, so instead of crashing into him and causing him a lot of pain and suffering, Yvonne had driven her car straight through him. Opening his eyes, Chris looked around and saw her turn round and prepare to try again.

Thinking quickly, Chris took control of the grass in the field, and immediately huge strands of it erupted out of the ground, enormous green shoots and leaves the size of enormous snakes that began wrapping around Yvonne's car.

Soon the vehicle was a writhing green mass, more and more of it piling on. Chris made the grass tighten, crushing the car in its grip. He heard the smash of glass and the grind of crunching metal as the grass squeezed like the coils of a python. When he was sure it had done all it could, Chris disbanded the vines of vegetation and went to peer into the car's shattered windows.

Yvonne wasn't there.

He heard a noise and looked behind him. And cursed.

A gigantic green tentacle made entirely of grass had risen out of the ground like an enormous worm and was now shooting towards him with lightning speed. Before he could do anything it wrapped him in its grip and lifted him high into the air. He felt it squeezing, and as he dangled helplessly he heard a sickening crack that might have been his ribs.

Fortunately, he remembered his Surviving Magic assessment with the fire kraken. Summoning his last reserves of strength Chris burst into flames. They spread onto the grass arm, which writhed as if hurt and let go, allowing Chris to gently float to the ground. But he was still on fire, and the pain of his rapidly healing ribs made him angry.

He launched a great wave of fire at the grass monstrosity, causing it to erupt in flames as they licked across it and completely covered it. The blazing column crumpled, and then rose up again into a monstrous fiery version of Yvonne, glaring down at him like a huge fiery demon.

Chris banished his own flames and blasted a sheet of water at her. The water enveloped Yvonne's inferno, submerging it in liquid until the fire was gone and there was nothing left of it. But just as Chris thought he was safe the water was thrown aside and Yvonne stood there facing him, an expression of intense fury on her beautiful face.

Chris made a split second decision that discretion was most definitely the better part of valour.

He turned and ran across the field, not stopping when he reached the motorway but flying into the air above the cars. Yvonne was not far behind him. Rather than fly after him she blasted a bolt of lightning at him. It knocked him out of the air and sent him crashing to the ground.

He did not have time to gather his strength for there were cars all around him going so fast that a collision with just one of them would have been fatal to a mortal. Chris dodged through the cars zooming past him whilst all the time aware that Yvonne was somewhere behind him.

Yvonne meanwhile, decided to take a less subtle approach. She strode into the motorway and cast a force field around herself so that any car that threatened to run her over was thrown into the air. Several cars met with her force field and were launched into the air to come crashing down in the path of the cars behind them. By the time Yvonne reached the barrier separating the two sections there was a huge pileup behind her.

She saw that Chris had made it to the field on the other side and with a determined look in her eye she flew into the air, forgetting to maintain her shield, straight into the path of an oncoming lorry.

Chris winced at the crunch and saw the lorry continue on into the distance. For a minute he sat down panting, completely exhausted. But then he thought of what might happen if Yvonne should return and catch him in this weakened state, so he summoned the last of his strength and used it to transport himself back to Lucy's house.

Chris found himself back in Lucy's bedroom. Lucy was asleep in her bed, and Chris knew by instinct the lamp was where he'd left it. He didn't know when Yvonne would get back, but didn't rate his chances of winning another contest with her. Still, before he made his next move he wanted to find some answers. The first place to look would be the attic, where Lucy had found his lamp in the first place. As he climbed the stairs to the attic Chris had a very nasty thought.

Yvonne had recognised him when she first saw him at the school. She seemed to know he was a genie. Perhaps the lamp being in the house of a fairy wasn't merely a coincidence. Could she have had something to do with his imprisonment in the lamp all those weeks ago? Saving these thoughts for later, Chris began looking around the attic for something, anything that might give him some idea as to what Yvonne wanted with Lucy.

The books were mainly old novels, with authors ranging from Charles Dickens through Jane Austen to Emile Zola. The photo albums all seemed to be of just Lucy and Yvonne, plus a few friends and/or relatives. But as Chris was putting the albums back in the box he had found them in, he noticed something lying hidden behind the box.

Two sheets of paper, one of them a photo and the other some sort of legal document. The photo was pretty old, and it must have been lying there for years because the dust on it was so thick that at first Chris couldn't make it out. But after a quick dusting down, he saw there were two people in it. A man and a woman, standing with their arms around each other's shoulders. Chris noticed the woman looked remarkably like Lucy, and the man... Chris gasped.

He was younger, he was scruffier, but there was no mistaking it. The man in the picture was Mr Djinn.

Chris dropped the photo and looked at the other sheet. Dusting it off, he realised it was a birth certificate. And it belonged to Lucy! The full name read "Lucia Grace Dee", and the date of birth was thirteen years ago. The parent's names were "Diana Amelia Dee", date of death the same day as Lucy's birth, and "John Michael Dee" date of death six months earlier.

John Dee. Dee John. Djinn.

Mr Djinn was Lucy's father, and Yvonne or one of her associates must have been responsible for him becoming a genie.

Things were becoming more complicated by the minute. But Chris didn't want to be here when Yvonne got back and perhaps if Mr Djinn knew all this he could help figure out what she was up to. Closing his eyes and taking a deep breath, Chris pictured himself in the main corridor of the genie academy. A second later he was back in the magic tunnel.

'AAAAAAAAAAAAAAHHHHH......!'

The flash of light. The running figure falling. Insane laughter. Another figure, strolling into the light. Tall, thin, hair flowing down the shoulders. Hair that glints gold in the light of the sun.

Chris materialised, not actually in the main corridor,

but in mid-air above one of the staircases leading down to the main corridor. He wasn't aware of this soon enough to do anything, and it was some minutes before he finally came to rest at the foot of the stairs, with several bumps and bruises rapidly healing.

'Chris?' said a familiar voice above him. He looked up and recognised Joe. 'Did you grant the three wishes already?' asked Joe.

'Not yet. I'm just here on a visit. Where's Mr Djinn? I need to talk to him.'

'Probably in reception. Come on, I'll escort you there.' Joe gave him a hand up and they walked to reception together.

Chris walked in without bothering to knock. Mr Djinn was standing with Miss Sato.

He looked up in surprise but smiled when he saw it was Chris. 'Hello, Mr Forrester! Didn't expect to see you back so soon! How was your trip to the mortal world?'

'Complicated,' answered Chris. 'I need to talk to you in private.'

'Very well. Mr Edgar, would you leave us please?'

'But…' protested Joe.

'*Now.*'

'Yes sir,' said Joe reluctantly, shutting the door as he left.

'Miss Sato can stay.' said Mr Djinn, nodding to the secretary. 'She's more important than her job suggests. Whatever I hear, she hears,'

'On your own head.' replied Chris forebodingly. 'I'll

get straight to the point. The girl who rubbed my lamp and let me out has a fairy godmother.'

'Good lord,' exclaimed Mr Djinn. 'How do you know this?'

'My "mistress" Lucy told me herself. The fairy's a woman calling herself Yvonne. I had a bit of a scrap with her earlier and witnessed her powers firsthand. Afterwards I went looking for something that could give me a clue as to what she's doing. I found Lucy's birth certificate. Her surname's Dee.'

Something Chris couldn't interpret appeared in Mr Djinn's expression.

'She's the daughter of a Diana Dee and a... John Dee.' Chris fell silent. Mr Djinn turned away and stared out the window at the cloudscape.

'The girl, Lucy, What was she like?' he asked, still facing the window.

'Thirteen years old,' answered Chris. 'Nice girl. Bit bossy, but there you go. I found a photo of her parents. She looks just like her mum.'

'Are they still alive? Her parents?'

'No. The birth certificate said her mum died the day Lucy was born. I assume it was in childbirth. As for the dad...'

Chris and Miss Sato exchanged glances.

At last Mr Djinn turned back round. He raised his eyes to meet those of Chris.

'I remember,' he declared.

'How?' asked Miss Sato.

'I always knew my name was John Dee, I changed it because I believed it was unhealthy to dwell on what I might have left behind. But many times during these last few years, the name Diana has appeared in my head, and I could never place who it belonged to. Now I know at last. And it's bringing back so many memories!'

'So what do you remember?' asked Chris.

'We met at university, Diana and I. My degree was in science, hers in history. We were married for five years. I can still remember the wedding: the 3rd of July; the service was held at the top of a hill. We could see the whole town spread out beneath us, it was so clear, and so sunny. Of course it was after that we moved to London. We were overjoyed when we found out Diana was pregnant. I was so looking forward to being a father. But I missed the birth. It looks as if I didn't even get to say goodbye to her.'

Miss Sato put an arm around the man's shoulders. Chris could see the tears in his eyes.

'Can you remember what happened? How you became a genie?' he asked gently. Mr Djinn shook his head. 'I can only remember up to a few days before it happened. That's all.'

'Mr Djinn, this is important. If you can remember how it happened you might recall some detail that could tell us what Yvonne's been up to all this time.'

'I can't. I don't know anyone called Yvonne. If I saw her perhaps I'd recognise her, but right now it's all a blank. I'm sorry Chris.'

'It's not your fault, John.' said Miss Sato. 'It's hers. That damned fairy. She's ruined a lot of lives through whatever she's planning. It's the same with every person or creature that turns someone into a genie. They cause such distress and sadness through that one deed. We all have people we left behind, who are still missing us, or worse, died never knowing what happened to us. But we genies stick together. We're there for each other. And nothing will change that.'

'Amen to that,' murmured Chris.

At that moment he felt a familiar feeling. He looked down and saw his body was glowing. It was happening again.

'Mr Djinn!' He jumped up and held out his hand to the headmaster. 'I'm being summoned. Come with me.'

'That's impossible!' protested Mr Djinn.

'She's your daughter, Mr Djinn. Yvonne's using her for something, and I think the rest of your memory might be the key to finding out what it is. A meeting with Lucy *and* Yvonne might just open that locked door in your mind. So what do you say?'

Mr Djinn looked at Chris' hand held out to him. Then he looked at Chris and smiled. 'I always did love a challenge.'

He took Chris' hand and they both vanished in a flash of light. 'AAAAAAAAAAAAAAHHHHH......!'

Mind Reader

Lucy held the lamp in her hand. It was still night outside and she was in her pyjamas. But she wanted a chat with Chris and when she rubbed it she was expecting him to come flying out the way he had when she first found it. She wasn't expecting him to have a companion.

Both Chris and Mr Djinn flew out of the lamp in a burst of light and went careering into the bed. They then rolled off it, taking the quilt and the pillows with them.

'Ouch. I'm never doing that again,' groaned Mr Djinn, getting to his feet alongside Chris. He then saw Lucy.

'Who are you?' demanded Lucy.

'Oh boy,' muttered Chris. 'Lucy, I'm not quite sure how to say this, but... this is your dad. Your real dad.'

Lucy and Mr Djinn stared at each other.

'That's impossible.' said Lucy. 'He's dead. My dad died in a fire before I was born.'

'Was his body found?' asked Chris.

'Well no. That is, they couldn't find what was left of him. But everyone knew he was in there. Yvonne said...'

'I'm afraid Yvonne lied to you. I expect there was a fire, but he wasn't killed. He was turned into a genie like me.'

'Yvonne wouldn't lie!' But Lucy's voice no longer

sounded certain.

'Do you have a picture of your parents?'

'One. I keep it under my pillow.' Chris looked under the only pillow that hadn't been knocked off the bed. Beneath it was a photo similar to the one he'd discovered in the attic. It was of Mr Djinn and Lucy's mother. Chris took it to Lucy and showed it to her.

Lucy just looked from it to Mr Djinn and back again, speechless.

Mr Djinn went up to her. 'All these years you've grown up never knowing what sort of a person your father was, or even what it was like to have a father. And for thirteen years I never knew I had a daughter somewhere. I didn't even remember having a wife. Your mother, your *real* mother, died thinking her husband was dead, thinking the baby she gave birth to would grow up an orphan. Now we all know better. My daughter. Oh my god!'

Father and daughter threw their arms around each other, and for the first time in a while Chris found himself wiping at his eyes.

Just then, an interruption occurred in the form of Yvonne barging in dressed in a nightmarish pink dressing gown.

'Lucy, why is your light on? It's almost two in the...' She took in the scene of Lucy and Mr Djinn standing side by side with Chris sat on the bed. She stared at Mr Djinn. 'It's not possible!' she exclaimed.

'My god!' said Mr Djinn, instantly recognising Yvonne. 'It's *you*! I remember now!'

'Then remember *this*!' And Yvonne threw a burst of lightning at Mr Djinn too suddenly for him to react. He was blasted straight through the wall and into the next room with a crash.

Chris hurled a fireball at her but she deflected it with ease and then pointed a finger at him. It was if a hand had closed over his throat. Struggling to breathe, he was lifted off his feet and suspended in the air.

'This is the third time you've got in my way!' Yvonne snarled, still pointing at him. 'I thought I was rid of you the first time! I thought imprisoning you in a lamp would get you out of my sight! It seems I reckoned without Lucy finding you!'

'Stop it!' cried Lucy. Yvonne glared at her for a minute and then released Chris. He fell to the floor, gasping for breath. '*You* made me a genie?' he repeated when he had regained his breath.

'Of course! When I saw you at the school I feared the worst, but as you didn't remember what I'd done to you, I assumed Lucy must have released you and made you her slave! But then you had to keep interfering! It seems you're not quite as obedient as most genies. And now you've gone and brought her father back! This is exactly why I usually kill my enemies! Whenever I spare them they keep coming back to haunt me!'

'Why didn't you tell me?' demanded Lucy. 'You said my dad died before I was born!'

'Lucy, dear, that was for your own protection. Protection from useless, stupid, interfering mortals! Oh,

Chris, you can look at me like I'm a monster, but who brought her up? I did! When her good-for-nothing father allowed himself to be imprisoned in his genie netherworld and her good-for-nothing mother went and died! I fed her, clothed her and nursed her! Not them! Who's the good parent now?'

'But why do it in the first place?' demanded Chris.

'Oh now, that would be telling.'

'She's not your daughter.' croaked a voice behind them.

They all turned and saw Mr Djinn staggering towards them, glaring at Yvonne. 'She's mine, and always will be. And I won't let you use her any longer.' He burst into flames and flew straight at Yvonne.

Before she could defend herself he barrelled into her and they both crashed into the wall. 'GO!' yelled Mr Djinn as he held onto the fairy.

'We're not leaving you!' protested Chris.

'GO NOW!'

With a last desperate look at Mr Djinn, Chris and Lucy both fled. As they ran, a fiery light lit the walls and Mr Djinn's scream echoed in their ears.

They charged into the attic and slammed the door shut. 'We can't leave him there!' said Lucy.

'He attacked Yvonne to buy us time! We can help him later. Right now, let's just concentrate on helping ourselves.' replied Chris.

'Well where do we go then?'

'You tell me. I could teleport us out of here but I

wouldn't know where I was going. And going to the Genie Academy wouldn't help; there are only so many genies we could drag back with us. A handful of genies wouldn't be any better match for a fairy than I was. And then of course there's the danger that Yvonne could follow us to Genie Academy. Tell you what!' Chris grinned at Lucy. 'Let's go for a flight!'

'Sorry?'

Instead of answering, Chris looked down at the carpet he and Lucy were standing on. 'Just watch this,' he said to her. Then he held his hands out, palms facing the floor. He flexed his fingers, and each time he uncurled them the carpet moved ever so slightly. Gradually it started to move more powerfully, and before long the whole thing was suspended in midair.

'You've got to be joking,' exclaimed Lucy. Chris jumped onto the carpet. He held out his hand to Lucy. 'Coming for a ride?' he asked. Warily, Lucy took his hand and climbed on behind him.

'Hold on!' cried Chris, then the carpet shot up, bursting through the roof and up into the sky.

The city disappeared beneath them until they were flying above the clouds, the stars and moon shining down upon them from the expanse of space under which they flew.

'Ladies and gentlemen, we are beginning our descent! Please fasten your seatbelts!' announced Chris.

'We haven't got any seatbelts!' replied Lucy.

'That's part of the fun!' laughed Chris, then the carpet

shot downwards again. Lucy clung on to Chris as the carpet raced along like a rollercoaster ride. They disturbed a flock of geese, narrowly avoided colliding with a plane, swooped down over the houses of Parliament, past the London Eye and then left the city behind, doing a barrel roll as they shot over the river Thames. At which point Chris was sick over the side.

'I've just remembered, I have travel sickness,' he informed Lucy after wiping his mouth.

'Bit late now,' replied Lucy, smirking.

Back at Lucy's home, Yvonne chained Mr Djinn to a chair with unbreakable bonds.

'Let's see you get out of that,' she jeered at him. He was still weak and battered after his fight with her. 'And even if you did, I've got this.' She showed him a ring on her left hand.

'This just happens to be what I imprisoned you in, thirteen years ago. And we both know that the only way to kill a genie is to destroy their prison. Sadly your young friend Chris took his lamp with him, so I can't do the same with him. But never mind. I have a way to get my daughter...'

'*My* daughter!' corrected Mr Djinn. Yvonne slapped him round the face.

'Don't interrupt! I have a way to get my daughter back and be rid of Chris.'

Yvonne turned her face upwards. Then she opened her mouth and let out a horrible piercing shriek. From elsewhere, that cry was echoed by more than one voice, and then the walls caved in and a flock of winged creatures burst through.

Yvonne smiled at them. 'Hello, my darlings. There's something I want you to do for me. You're going to enjoy it very much.'

In the sky, Chris and Lucy were now just gently cruising along on the carpet. There was nothing but fields and trees below them, and the occasional farm.

'So, any idea where to go?' asked Lucy.

'Not really,' answered Chris. 'I may just find somewhere quiet where we can think.'

'Thinking is all we can do right now, I suppose.'

'My thoughts exactly.'

Both teenagers were silent for a moment.

'So Yvonne's been using me all this time,' said Lucy quietly.

'Certainly seems so,' replied Chris.

'But what could she want with me?'

'I wish I knew.' They fell silent again. Neither of them felt like talking. Up until now Chris had always known he had the genies to go to for help should he ever need it, but now he couldn't risk it. He was also beginning to feel the weight of responsibility given that he now had to keep Lucy safe.

Lucy was equally unhappy. She had just discovered her adoptive mother was the reason she had grown up an orphan and while she had just found her father he was in trouble and she had no idea how to save him. Lucy wondered if she was ever going to get a good night's sleep.

Absentmindedly, she looked behind them. A strange cloud in the distance caught her eye. Looking closer, she realised it was moving too fast to be a cloud.

'Chris!' She pointed at the cloud. Chris turned and stared at them. The cloud was getting nearer, and they could just make out lots of winged creatures flying together in a swarm. Recognition dawned on Chris as he saw their bat-like appearances. 'Banshees.' he exclaimed.

'What?'

'Banshees,' They're like parasites. They're invisible to mortals. They feed on life force, usually preying on dying creatures. There's an old legend that sometimes people hear them screeching and know that someone's died. But why are they coming after us?'

'Yvonne must have sent them!' suggested Lucy.

'How on earth did she get the services of banshees?'

'And there's one more thing.'

'What?'

'If mortals can't see them, how come I can see them?'

Chris looked at her, and she met his gaze. 'Ah,' he replied, 'Good question.'

The cloud headed ever closer, and they could hear the snarls and screeches of the banshees. 'Hold on, I'm going to see if we can outrun them!' said Chris, and the carpet accelerated.

But the banshees were fast, and were still catching up.

Chris tried to shake them off by performing quick changes of direction and sudden bursts of speed, but the banshees never seemed to lose them. Then, as the carpet was racing along and the banshees were close behind them, another cloud of the creatures appeared directly in front of them. Chris tried to brake but it was too late and they collided with the swarm.

In the nick of time Chris summoned a lightning shield that encircled the carpet and electrocuted any banshee that tried to break through. The carpet barrelled through them, causing angry screeches and snarls. However, the banshees were cleverer than they looked.

After several minutes of individual ones trying to break through and failing, they quickly reformed into a huge swarm and all dived in at once. The impact caused Chris to lose control of the shield and it collapsed.

The banshees were all over them in a second, grabbing at them, tearing at the carpet, trying to pull them off. Thinking quickly, Chris grabbed Lucy's hand, closed his eyes and exploded. This was a trick Mr Djinn had taught him in Performing Magic class, but he had never tried one this big.

The burst of heat and light incinerated the banshees and the carpet in a huge fireball, before shrinking again to form Chris, eyes closed and hand still clinging onto Lucy to protect her. Unfortunately the carpet was now no more and there was nothing between them and the ground nine hundred feet below.

'Chris!' cried Lucy.

Chris came to his senses and they both came to a halt, floating in midair. 'I'm not doing that again,' muttered Chris. 'Does my head in.'

A surviving banshee swooped at them from out of nowhere, colliding with Chris and causing him to let go of Lucy's hand. Lucy immediately started falling with a scream, whilst Chris was pulled to earth by the banshee.

Landing, the banshee then put its hand on Chris' chest and began to drain him. Chris knew what it was doing. It was eating his life force, draining every last drop. Of course, it wouldn't kill him. He was a genie, he had unlimited amounts of life force, so the banshee would probably keep drinking until it exploded. But that wouldn't help Lucy.

Chris could see her out of the corner of his eye, plummeting to earth. It was his fault.

He had to go and get involved, and now they were being decimated by a psycho fairy and an army of renegade banshees.

As his life force continued to ebb away, and darkness flickered at the edges of his vision, Chris suddenly felt angry. Angrier than he had ever felt before. Fierce, raging fury blazed at the very heart of his soul. And at that moment it erupted. Something deep in the nether regions of his magic was unlocked, and a terrible power no genie had ever possessed before exploded straight out from inside Chris' body in a blinding flash of crimson red lightning that threw the banshee off him and blasted it to the ground, where it lay still.

Chris lay there, panting. And he looked at the banshee.

He knew what he'd done, but he just couldn't believe it. The banshee's body began to crumble into ash, the life force it had taken in its lifetime going out like a candle. Chris had done what no genie had done since the first genie was created. He had killed.

Lucy's scream brought him back to his senses. With the speed of thought, he brought her to a halt only a few inches from the ground, and levitated her over to where he sat. She landed beside him, a bit breathless but more or less intact. She stared at the banshee's remains. 'What happened to it?' she asked.

'Don't know,' Chris lied. 'Must have overindulged itself.'

Lucy looked at him disbelievingly but said nothing. They sat together in the field with a full moon shining down upon them.

Eventually, Chris turned to Lucy and said: 'Brace yourself Lucy, I'm going to try something only half reliable and potentially life threatening.'

'And what's that?' asked Lucy.

'I'm going to read your mind.'

'No thank you!' replied Lucy indignantly, 'My thoughts are private.'

'I know, but at the moment it seems to be the only thing that could work. Maybe there's some suppressed memory I could find which could give us a clue as to what Yvonne wants.'

Lucy still wasn't convinced. 'When you say potentially

life threatening…'

'Only hypothetically. But you needn't worry; I know how to do it.'

'Have you done it before?'

Chris thought for a minute. 'Well, not exactly…'

'What do you mean by "not exactly"?'

'At Genie Academy, because no-one can remember past the day they arrived, you don't have to go very deep in their mind before you find a door blocking you out. So I have done it, I just haven't done very high level mind reading. Trust me, you'll be fine.'

'Trust you?'

'Yes, *me*. Just close your eyes and clear your head.'

Lucy did as he said and Chris placed his hands on either side of her head, closing his own eyes. Lucy felt him leafing through her memories like pages in a book. Some he would barely glance at, others he would dwell on for longer. She found old memories being reawakened as he disturbed long-forgotten episodes in her childhood. Chris was careful not to focus on the less happy ones for too long, but they were still there, Lucy could feel them.

As she felt him wandering around in her head, she thought about what it would be like to read the mind of a genie.

'Since we're talking about memories, I never asked, what's it like to be unable to remember who you were before you were a genie?' she asked.

'Depends,' he replied quietly.

'On what?'

'On what kind of a mood I'm in. Sometimes it doesn't seem too bad. Other times I find myself remembering little details, like my favourite colour, my best subjects, but I'm unable to remember beyond that. Sometimes I picture a face, and I know I haven't met them at Genie Academy, so they must be from my old life, but I just can't remember who they are.'

Lucy could hear the frustration in his voice.

'It's maddening,' Chris continued. 'Especially when you lie awake at night thinking about it. Sometimes I even dream about the mortal world, and when I wake up I can't tell if the people and places and events in the dream are just figments of my imagination, or memories buried in my subconscious. Reading another genie's mind is like reading my own. Eventually there's just a door which won't open for me no matter how hard I push.'

Chris fell silent and continued reading Lucy's mind. Then he stopped on one memory which Lucy had long forgotten. 'Stonehenge?' murmured Chris. 'Why Stonehenge?' He let the memory play like a film reel. It was ten years ago, when Lucy was just three years old.

'Aww, weren't you a cute toddler?' cooed Chris.

'Oy!'

'Sorry.'

Yvonne had taken her there; she'd led her by the hand around the magnificent stone blocks. But it was busy that day, there were a lot of people, and in all the excitement Lucy's hand had slipped from Yvonne's and she was suddenly alone. But she hadn't cried. She had simply sat underneath one of the stone structures. A trapdoor had fallen open at her feet, as if inviting her to step inside. There was a flight of stone steps leading down and down into the darkness. Full of infant curiosity, she had wandered down the steps into the darkness and then...

Nothing. Just darkness. Darkness and then Lucy climbed up the steps and out into daylight.

And Yvonne had seen her, and ran over and gathered her up in her arms. And to this day, she had no recollection of what had happened in the underground passage. Chris' efforts had revealed nothing but darkness. Lucy could feel his frustration.

'What happened?' he grumbled to himself. 'That can't be it! What happened in the stupid chamber?'

'You're always so grumpy.' said Lucy.

'No I'm not!' Chris opened his eyes.

'I'm surprised your mum and dad put up with you. Although it seems you got it from your dad.'

'What did you say?'

'Your sister doesn't seem to be particularly cheerful either and... Wow, your friend Loki is really good looking...'

Chris took his hands from Lucy's head and stared at her. She opened her eyes and stared back.

'How did you do that?' Chris demanded.

'I don't know.'

'But that wasn't just simple mind reading, you managed to see inside the memories I can't remember, they weren't ones I've simply forgotten, they've been physically hidden from me! Not even a genie can see past them!'

'Is that good or bad?'

'I don't know, but it's definitely not natural. Why, you'd have to be...Ohhhh...' Realisation dawned on Chris' face.

'What?'

'Lucy, you're a Mind Reader. An actual, proper Mind Reader, with capital letters. That explains everything! The fact you can see banshees, like I said, no mortal can see them, but a Mind Reader isn't mortal! Not completely mortal, anyway. And the way you stopped my own magic killing me! You had to control my mind in order to control my magic!'

'So what's the difference between a Mind Reader and... a mind reader?'

'Well, any magic user can read minds if they try, genies, witches, fairies, but they can only read memories and thoughts. Actual Mind Readers can do all that, but they can control minds as well, and they can find memories long forgotten because of things like amnesia. The first time you did that thing with the magic, what happened?'

Lucy thought back to that day in primary school.

'Well, it wasn't actually magic,' she explained. 'There was a boy in school who'd fallen and cut his knee. I put my hand on the bad leg and he said it went numb.'

'Cutting off the leg's nerve sensors to the brain stopped the kid feeling anything. But Mr Djinn said only

106

one Mind Reader is born every generation.' said Chris thoughtfully.

'Could that be what Yvonne wants with me?'

'Could be. But what could she need that only a Mind Reader can do?'

Chris turned and looked straight at her. 'Stonehenge,' he breathed. 'It must be something to do with Stonehenge. Yvonne's looking for something underneath the Stonehenge circle. And she needs you to find it for her.'

'But if Yvonne wanted me to find this thing even before I was born, she must have known my mum would give birth to a Mind Reader. How could she have known that?'

Chris remembered his lessons with Mr Abdullah in History of Magic. 'Well, it's like the Muslim stories of the prophet Muhammad,' he explained. 'It was discovered that he was destined to be Allah's prophet when he was just a boy, because of certain markings on his body and other things. Well if you were looking for the parents of someone like him, you could go through the same procedure.'

'So, Yvonne was able to find the parents of the next Mind Reader?' asked Lucy.

'Supposedly,' answered Chris. 'But why did she wait so long? She's a fairy, she's immortal, so she could have done this with another Mind Reader centuries ago, why now?'

'More to the point, what does she want underneath Stonehenge?'

'Let's find out!' Chris gave her his hand. 'At least now I know where we're going!' Lucy took his hand and they both disappeared into thin air.

Lucy had never teleported before. Come to think of it, she'd never flown a carpet before; this was definitely her night for first experiences. Teleporting felt a bit like sliding down a slide in a playground. First the world dropped away and there was darkness, then you felt as if you were moving but your feet still felt connected to the ground. And then it stopped and the world revealed itself. Lucy found herself standing beside Chris with the Stonehenge circle in the background. It was still night time, and the silvery moonlight made the flat landscape rather eerie, especially with no-one else around.

'Now what?' asked Lucy.

'I don't know. I'm making this up as I go along,' replied Chris. 'Maybe if we find that passage you went inside when you were little we could find out what this is all about.'

He became aware of a sound, a siren-screeching-screaming sound, somewhere high above him but growing rapidly louder. It had a familiar ring…

'Er, Chris?' said Lucy.

'Yes?'

'Look up.'

Chris did as she said and realised why her voice had a chill to it. An immense cloud of banshees was blotting out the moonlight and closing in around them, blocking all escape routes and filling the night with the sounds of their screeches. A path opened up between them and Yvonne stepped out towards Chris and Lucy, dressed in another one of her glamorous outfits.

Chris held up a glowing hand and pointed it at her. 'Don't you come anywhere near us!' he snarled.

'What are you going to do, throw your hormones at me?' sneered Yvonne.

Then she made a quick motion with her hand and Chris' lamp flew from his pocket and into her hand.

'Hey!' protested Chris but before he could do anything Yvonne pressed a burning finger against the lamp. Excruciating pain ripped through Chris' body and he dropped to the ground in agony.

'There's an annoying thing about genies that makes them keep on reappearing no matter how many times you defeat them,' said Yvonne as she removed her finger. 'But if you happen to possess their lamp, there's no end to what you can do!' She prodded the lamp again and Chris cried out.

'Destroy the prison and you destroy the prisoner!' taunted Yvonne. 'But why kill when you can have so much more fun making them suffer?'

And she continued the torture, burning the lamp for longer each time, until Lucy ran up to her and snatched the lamp out of her hands. Yvonne glared at her and held out her hand. 'Give it back, Lucy.' The girl didn't move. 'I said give it *back*!' Yvonne threw a shock wave at Lucy that knocked her off her feet, making her drop the lamp. Yvonne grabbed it and turned to the banshees.

'Take him and chain him up with the other genie! I'll deal with them later!'

The banshees obeyed and carried the unresisting Chris to the other side of the circle, where Mr Djinn had suddenly appeared, chained to one of the structures. Yvonne had hidden him with an invisibility shield until now.

Yvonne and Lucy were now on their own. The fairy offered her hand to Lucy who ignored it and got up by herself.

'You're not going to hold this against me, are you?' asked Yvonne.

'What do you think? You've been lying to me all my life. You don't love me really.'

'Of course I love you! Surely you didn't think I was lying about that! I just need you to do one small thing for me, and then we can go back to the way we were before.' Yvonne was acting as if she had been perfectly reasonable, but Lucy wasn't convinced.

'I won't do it,' she said, and her tone implied she meant it.

'At least let me explain,' said Yvonne. 'Do you know why the Stonehenge circle was built? It was built to house a weapon. We don't know a lot about it, but there are ancient scriptures written by witches and wizards from millennia ago, saying that a race of elves built something of phenomenal power, and they buried it here. Apparently its power scared them, so they hid it where no-one but the elves could find it. This structure is designed to block out anyone that tries to look for the weapon. But, here's the snag. This particular species of elves were Mind Readers, with skills far beyond any fairy or witch. They could use their incredible minds to locate the weapon and bring it out above ground.

'Unfortunately these elves died out long ago but some of them bred with humans and so, once every generation a human Mind Reader is born. You are a Mind Reader Lucy. I only found this out about the elves in the last few decades, and by then Mind Readers were hard to come by. Then I discovered your parents would give birth to one, and I thought by getting rid of your father and persuading your dying mother to make me your fairy godmother, I could bring you up as my own and train you for the moment your powers became fully developed, which always happens at the age of thirteen.

'I know you think ill of me for using you in this way, but I never meant you any harm. I always intended to tell you of your destiny before you came of age, but never found the right moment. And, from what I've read, this weapon could give the user enough power to rule the world. Find it, and I could give you everything you've ever wanted.

So will you do it?'

Lucy still didn't intend to do anything of the sort. 'Why should I help you?' she demanded.

'Well, I had hoped to persuade you with other means, but you've left me no choice. Follow me.' Yvonne led Lucy to another structure, where five people, three of them men and two women were chained up. 'Archaeologists.' said Yvonne. 'Come to start excavating again for the first time in fifty years. Unfortunately they decided to do their work just as I was ready to get on with this operation. I've always despised archaeologists. Now, I suggest you do as I say, or I'll give the order and my banshees will feed.'

'You wouldn't!'

'I would. I wouldn't think twice about it. But I'll spare them and your genie friends if you do this for me. Understand?'

'Exactly what would you do with this weapon thing?' demanded Lucy suspiciously.

'That's not your concern.'

'Not my concern? I'm the one getting it for you!'

'Remember, lives hang in the balance. Though to be fair, if I was in your position, I'd let the hostages die. But that's because unlike you I've had plenty of experience with killing.'

Lucy looked from the archaeologists to Chris and Mr Djinn and sighed. It was clear she didn't have much of a choice.

'What do you want me to do?' she asked at last.

'What you did last time. The weapon was calling to you even at that young age, but I knew you weren't ready. You're ready now. Fulfil your destiny!'

Lucy, still glaring at Yvonne with hatred, turned and headed towards the circle. When she reached one of the structures, a stairway opened up before her again. With one last look back, she descended into the darkness.

The Stonehenge Weapon

Underground, Lucy could see nothing but darkness. She had no sense of direction; there weren't even any walls to feel her way along. The stairs had gone, and now there was just her and the endless dark space. To stop her increasing feeling of claustrophobia she decided just to walk in a random direction. But she had only gone a few steps when she felt something holding her back. It wasn't a wall as such, more like a strong mental barrier that made her unable to go on. But she knew she had to, for everyone's sake.

Concentrating hard, she struggled against it, but no matter how hard she tried the barrier wouldn't yield. Then she remembered that she'd only ever used her mind powers when she was relaxed. So she took a deep breath and calmed down, then stepped forward. This time there was no resistance whatsoever, and not only did the barrier lift but her hands came into contact with stone. By feeling her way along the wall she found a small doorway into some sort of underground cave. Cautiously, Lucy entered the dark cavern.

As she walked in several torches lining the walls burst into blue flames and lit up the cave with an eerie flickering light. The cave was bare except for the torches and a large marble box resembling a coffin in the middle of the room. Lucy approached the coffin hesitantly, wondering if it contained the weapon she was looking for. But no sooner had she reached it than a sound came from inside, like something trying to break its way out.

A large crack appeared along the middle of the coffin, and with a sound like stone splitting the lid of the coffin burst in two and fell to the floor. A man sat up inside.

He looked human, but he was pale and gaunt and his hair hung long and white beneath a small silver crown which sat on his head between two abnormally pointed ears. He slowly got out of the coffin, a long grey cloak reaching to his feet, and Lucy saw he was very tall and wore clothes of an old design, rather like the kind of attire worn by Saxon kings. To complete the effect a huge sword with jewels encrusted in its hilt and scabbard hung from his belt.

The elf fixed Lucy with a penetrating gaze from his old, old eyes.

'I was not expecting a child.' he said in a cold, gravelly voice.

'Excuse me...' began Lucy.

'Don't interrupt.' commanded the elf. He said it very quietly but there was no mistaking the authority in his voice. He slowly approached Lucy, gazing at her thoughtfully. 'You are human, are you not?' he demanded.

'Yes sir.' answered Lucy.

'No human could have possibly got past the mental barriers present here. You must be something new.'

'I can explain...' said Lucy but the elf interrupted again.

'Explanation is not necessary; I can read your mind.' The elf closed his eyes. Lucy felt strange, as if something were attempting to get inside her head. It was like when Chris had read her mind only less gentle; it made her want to keep it out, to fight back. The elf's face screwed up with effort. Lucy felt the pressure on her mind increase and she had to fight harder to keep it from breaking through. At last the elf opened his eyes, breathing hard.

He glared at Lucy. 'Clearly this is no trick,' he concluded. 'You are a human with powers equal to mine, or they would be if you were older. But why have you come here?'

'I heard there was a weapon buried here,' explained Lucy. 'Someone sent me to find it.'

'Ah,' breathed the elf. He reached up a long, thin arm and snapped his fingers. Several feet from where Lucy was standing a crack appeared in the floor. Out of the ground rose a huge, golden pillar, rising up and up until it stood twice Lucy's height from the ground. At the very top of the pillar there sat a silver globe of metal, no bigger than a person's hand.

The elf reached up and gently picked it up and held it in front of his face, gazing at it in awe.

'The Elf Heart,' he said almost to himself. 'It contains the still-beating heart of an extremely powerful elf. The heart used to belong to a great elf king, called Mordred, who united us under one crown to fight a terrible war against the fairies long ago. But he had a deep secret. He was in love with the fairy queen, Guenhumara who was also his mortal enemy. No-one knows for sure how they met or how they conducted their love affair, but whatever the secrets in their relationship it ended in tragedy. The elves won the war but the fairy queen was killed. The king's heart was broken. It's extremely difficult to kill a fairy, but in the battle someone succeeded and he lost his lover forever.'

The elf's expression became very solemn, as if the story moved him as much as it had the king.

'In his grief he tore out his heart and died, but the heart carried on beating. And the elves realised just how powerful it was. All that emotion contained in one small object, they could use it to rule the world. For years it ensured the greatness of the elf empire, but then its power began to scare them. This can kill even an immortal; imagine what it could do in the hands of our enemies. So, in order to protect the world from it, the Elf Heart was placed underneath this stone structure, with a mental barrier guarding it.'

The elf drew himself up importantly.

'I, brother to the last king of this elf kingdom, was assigned to protect it with my life until such time as the elves should have need of it. But it's been so long now that I fear no elf will ever come for it. I am doomed to remain here until someone, anyone comes for it. No elf has lived as long as I have and look what it's done to me.' The elf examined his old and decrepit form bitterly. 'I was once the most handsome member of the royal family, and now I am no more youthful or energetic than a corpse. To guard the Elf Heart is both an honour and a curse.'

'I can take it from you,' said Lucy. The elf looked her over with disbelief.

'You are a mere mortal child, why should you be deserving of such a powerful weapon?' he demanded.

'Well, like you say, no-one would suspect me of possessing such a powerful object, so it would be safe with me.'

The elf laughed a cracked and throaty noise that made Lucy's hair stand on end. A look came into his eye that she did not like. 'You're not getting away that easily,' said the elf, still laughing. 'If you wish to take the Elf Heart from this place you must prove yourself worthy.'

'How do I do that?' asked Lucy.

In answer, the elf launched a mental shock wave at Lucy that knocked her off her feet.

'I am the most powerful Mind Reader alive.' said the elf. 'To prove yourself worthy you must defeat me!' He sent another mental wave that sent Lucy flying straight into the wall at the far end of the cavern. She crashed into the stone and fell to the floor amid a shower of rubble.

Shakily, she got to her feet, a determined look in her eye. She summoned up the most powerful mental wave she could muster and sent it straight at the elf. He batted it aside as if it were a clumsy insect and retaliated. Lucy tried to prepare herself but the force of her shock wave had weakened her and she was once again thrown

117

violently to the ground.

'You are weak,' growled the elf, picking her up with his mind and slamming her against the wall. The wind was knocked out of her and she dropped limply to the floor.

'You cannot hope to harness the power of the Elf Heart if you cannot withstand an attack from me!' snarled the elf as he launched another shock wave that sent Lucy spinning head-over-heels across the cave.

She came to rest against the pillar. She looked up at the elf, glaring down at her contemptuously. Lucy was battered and bruised, but she was also very, very angry.

'What possible match are you for...'

The elf did not finish his sentence for Lucy caught him by surprise with an extremely strong shock wave that sent him flying across the cave straight into the wall. He fell to the ground and lay still.

For a minute Lucy was worried that she might have badly hurt him, but he slowly got to his feet, clapping. For the first time, Lucy saw him smile. 'Well done,' he said, picking up the Elf Heart. 'You have proved yourself a true Mind Reader, and it is my honour and privilege to present this to you.' He offered her the Elf Heart. Lucy took it hesitantly. It was not very big, but such was the power contained inside that it was very heavy. She pressed it to her ear and heard, deep inside, the sound of a heart beating.

'Thank you,' she said to the elf.

'But be careful with it,' he warned her. 'You hold in your hand an object of immense power. Treasure it, but never trust it, for no-one can truly control a broken heart.'

'I promise,' said Lucy. She turned to go, and then turned back to the elf. 'What will you do?' she asked.

The elf sighed. 'I've spent most of the last few thousand years asleep; a bit more won't hurt. By the way, what is your name?'

'Lucy.'

'My name is Arthur. Farewell, Lucy. You have shown that you are deserving of the power of a Mind Reader.'

'Goodbye. And thank you.' Lucy offered him her hand. Arthur looked from it to her blankly. 'You shake it.' explained Lucy.

'I see.' Arthur shook her hand suspiciously.

Lucy then bid him a last goodbye and walked out of the cave with the Elf Heart in her hand. Looking back, she saw Arthur climb back into the stone coffin, which began to reassemble its pieces until it looked as if it had never broken. Then she headed back towards the shaft of moonlight illuminating the stairs.

Directly above, Chris sat next to Mr Djinn chained to one of the stone pillars. The chains of course were unbreakable and in any case they were both still very weak from Yvonne's torture. They were being guarded by banshees, who spent most of their time glaring hungrily at them. Chris could understand why, since as far as life force went, he and Mr Djinn were all-you-can-eat buffets. Just when he thought things couldn't get worse, Yvonne strode up to them. She smiled at them smugly, holding up their lamp and ring.

'Just in case you're thinking of trying to escape.' she gloated. 'Although you can't, because your chains are unbreakable. Shame, that.'

'Where's Lucy?' demanded Mr Djinn.

'Fulfilling her destiny. Retrieving the ultimate weapon for me. I'd get it myself but only a Mind Reader can find it,' answered Yvonne.

'That's your thirteen-year-plan?' said Chris. 'To find some stupid weapon? Why go to all this trouble?'

'You really have no idea, do you?' said Yvonne. She crouched down until her face was level with Chris, putting the lamp down.

'War is coming, boy. And not just one of your petty human scraps. This one will bring every race on earth, magical and non-magical, into the ultimate conflict. The stars have foreseen it, and we need to prepare ourselves. The Stonehenge weapon will make the fairies invincible.'

'Sounds like warmongering to me,' said Chris.

'Jeer all you want. You can't escape fate. Even the banshees know what's coming, and I promised them an alliance with the fairies if they agreed to serve me. Now if you'll excuse me, I need to check on Lucy.'

As she turned to leave, Chris said: 'You still haven't told me why you made me a genie.' Yvonne stopped and turned back to him.

'I haven't, have I? Then let me enlighten you.' She crouched down before him. 'But why should I waste my breath talking? Let me show you.' She placed her hand on his forehead and Chris gasped as the memories came flooding back.

Chris and his friend Loki had been in London on a day trip. The train back home had been delayed and Chris volunteered to go and get them something to eat. First he had to pass through an alleyway. It was dark save for dim sunlight creeping in. He saw two figures, one running and the other standing still. The still person raised their hand and there was a flash of light. The runner fell to the floor, the purse he had stolen dropping from his hand.

Laughter, and then a tall blonde woman walked into the light. Chris ran, not stopping, until he crashed into someone who held onto him. Chris struggled blindly until the person spoke.

'Chris?' said a familiar voice. Chris saw it was the tall, dark-haired young man called Loki.

'Where have you been?' Loki supported him as Chris slumped in his arms.

'Loki?'

'Yes Chris?'

'I need your help.'

Chris led him to the alleyway where he had seen the murder. To Chris' shock, the woman was still there, but the body was nowhere to be seen. They followed her through the streets until they came to a house, where the two of them hid themselves and watched her go in. At Chris' urging, though he had not told Loki of what he had seen, they made their way to her house together and knocked on the door. Yvonne answered it. She looked at them questioningly. Chris swallowed. 'Could I speak to you please?' he asked cautiously. Yvonne, looking suspicious, invited them in. She took them to her living room and bade them sit down. There was evidence that she didn't live alone, photographs of her with a girl not much younger than themselves. But whoever this girl was, she wasn't there at present.

'And what can I do for you?' asked Yvonne.

Chris took a deep breath. 'I saw you kill a man'

Loki stared at him in amazement. Yvonne merely raised an eyebrow.

'Oh?' she said.

'There was a man,' explained Chris. 'He stole your purse and you... did something. And he fell. He didn't look alive.'

'That is a very serious allegation.' Said Yvonne.

'That is an understatement.' muttered Loki.

'Have you any proof?' asked Yvonne.

'No.' answered Chris. 'But I think you should go to the police and turn yourself in. If you said it was self-defence...'

'I can assure you I have no intention of doing anything of the sort.'

'In that case I have no choice but to...'

'To what? Tell the police? Look at you, you're a schoolboy. They'll never believe a word of it.'

'I'll still do it.'

'Yvonne stood up. 'If you think I'm going to let you,

you snivelling little wretch…'

'Don't call him that!' snapped Loki, also standing up.

'Or what?!' demanded Yvonne.

'Now then, said Chris, also getting to his feet. Then Yvonne did something. There was a flash of light and Chris was on the floor. Darkness.

'Chris?' said Loki, crouching over him. 'Look at me, Chris. Chris, it's Loki.' Chris's eyes opened slightly and moaned. Loki got up, glaring at Yvonne. 'What have you done to him?' he hissed.

'Given him what he deserves.' Replied Yvonne. She made a movement with her hand and Loki froze, unable to move. She looked at them both. 'Another murder may be one too many.' She said, almost to herself. 'I shall simply get rid of you both. You,' she looked at Loki. 'Somewhere far away where no-one will ever find you.' She pointed at him and he disappeared in an explosion of bright colours. Yvonne turned to Chris' recumbent form. 'And you will be kept right here where I can keep an eye on you.' She made another movement with her hands and Chris' body diminished to a tiny flicker of light that flew straight into a lamp sitting on the mantelpiece. And there the memory ended.

Chris came to his senses. He was still where he was, with Yvonne in front of him. She took her hand from his head.

'What did you do with Loki?' demanded Chris.

'That's none of your concern. You should never have

poked your nose into my business in the first place, and then you'd still be living a normal human life at home.'

Yvonne turned to walk away.

'Anyway,' she said looking back with that same gleeful smile. 'I've rambled on long enough. You just sit there and reflect on the shambles that is your life and I'll see how Lucy's doing.'

And with that the fairy exited, leaving Chris to do exactly what she said.

Lucy sat on the ground next to the captive archaeologists. Yvonne now had the Elf Heart. Lucy had given it to her the moment she stepped out of the passage under the circle. She'd had no choice. Yvonne had then brought her here, assuring her no harm would come to her or the other hostages if she behaved herself. Then the fairy had left with the Elf Heart. Lucy had never felt so helpless.

She had no means of escape, two banshees were watching her, and even if she could escape there was just open countryside for miles. And she couldn't guarantee the safety of Chris and the others if she tried to escape.

Chris and her father were chained on the other side of the circle from her. She couldn't get to them and couldn't get a message to them without the banshees seeing. Lucy had only just met Mr Djinn but she already missed him, and as for Chris… well, he could be a bit of a show-off but he hadn't let her down so far. Not a lot at least.

As she was thinking about this Lucy had an idea.

Yvonne may have been in possession of Chris' lamp, but Lucy was the one who had let him out. And he hadn't yet granted all her wishes.

Closing her eyes, Lucy said to herself: 'Chris, I wish you could free yourself.'

On the other side of the circle, Chris felt his chains slacken, and with a quick movement he managed to blast them open. The banshees leapt at him but he stunned them both.

'I'll come back for you.' he whispered, and Mr Djinn nodded. Then Chris ran across to Lucy.

The banshees guarding her were also finished off without too much mess.

'Listen, Yvonne's got the weapon!' said Lucy.

'I kind of guessed that. What is the thing anyway?'

'It's called the Elf Heart. Long story. Any idea how we can get out of here?'

Chris scratched his head thoughtfully. 'Well I could probably teleport us all out, but I expect Yvonne would find us eventually.'

'What if we go to Genie Academy?'

'Well, we'll need my lamp first it's the only way to get there.' He snapped his fingers with delight. 'Yvonne left it behind when she was talking to me! If I can get to the school, all the genies can cast a transportation spell together and come here. A few hundred banshees will be no match for a thousand genies!'

'Well you'd better get going then!'

Chris looked at Lucy uncertainly. 'What will you do?'

'Get this lot away of course! Can't stay here if there's going to be violence!'

'I don't know how long it'll take to cast a transportation spell, especially with organising every genie in the school first! We may not get here in time.'

'You'll just have to hurry up, then!'

Chris sighed. By now he knew now that there was no stopping Lucy when her mind was set on something.

'Fine,' he said. 'Here, I'll just free these guys. Somehow I doubt Yvonne would use unbreakable chains on archaeologists.'

Sure enough, the chains came off with a quick flare of fire. The other captives shook themselves free.

'Good luck!' said Chris.

'You too,' replied Lucy.

Chris ran to where Mr Djinn was and picked up his lamp from where it lay on the grass. Then he turned to Mr Djinn. 'Where's your ring?' he asked.

'Yvonne took it with her. I think she's still a little fond of her jewellery,' answered Mr Djinn.

'I can take you with me then, that's how we got here!'

'She'd kill me with the ring when she discovered we were both gone. Trust me, it's safer if you go on your own,' replied Djinn calmly.

'I can't just leave you here.'

Mr Djinn smiled at him. 'You have to. I've said it before Chris; you're a far more powerful genie than I could ever hope to be. I have faith in you. Now go and rally the troops. I'm going to need their help. And another thing, how on earth did you learn to kill?'

'I don't know; it just seems to be something I can do when I'm in great danger, or someone else is.'

The headmaster raised an eyebrow. 'Someone else?'

'Someone I like.'

Mr Djinn gave him a strange look.

'Like. Hmm. Well you'd better tell that to the genies, because they may need the killing spell later on. I'll try and free myself, though it may take a while. Now go and make me proud, Chris Forrester.'

'Yes sir.' And with that, Chris disappeared in the same colourful flash of light.

'AAAAAAAAAAAAAAHHHHH......!!!'

The Battle of Stonehenge

He landed with a splash in the fountain in the main corridor. Gasping and spluttering, he clambered out and dried himself off with a quick spell. 'So there you are!' exclaimed Miss Sato when she entered the corridor and saw him. 'I've been worried sick! And where's Mr Djinn?'

'I'll explain later. Listen, I need you to call every genie in the school and have them go outside. Something big has happened and I need to talk with everyone!'

The secretary nodded and ran inside the reception office. A moment later, her amplified voice sounded on the intercom: 'Will all genies please congregate outside the school gates. This is an emergency. Repeat: all genies congregate outside the school.'

Outside, Chris saw an enormous crowd of genies, young and old from countries all over the world stretching across the cloudscape. Chris levitated three feet in the air and amplified his voice: 'Can I have your attention please?'

Gradually, all eyes turned towards him. 'I'm afraid something rather bad has happened.'

'Too right! Where the hell's Mr Djinn?' shouted someone in the crowd. Other people murmured in agreement.

'He's being held prisoner by a fairy!' answered Chris.

'The fairies don't kidnap genies! They've been at peace with all other magical creatures for centuries!' said someone else.

'This one's a psychopath!' replied Chris. 'Anyway that's not the point! This fairy has found the lost weapon of Stonehenge! It's something called the Elf Heart and apparently it can make the user all-powerful!'

'So what do you want us to do?' asked Joe.

'If we all cast a transportation spell at once, the sheer amount of magic could take us all to Stonehenge!' explained Chris. 'Trust me; the fairy has an army of banshees helping her, it'll take all of us to stop her!'

'It'll never work! The only way to get to the mortal world is if you're summoned!' shouted someone.

'Has anyone ever tried a mass transportation spell?' demanded Chris. There were a few murmurs but no direct answer. 'Then how do you know it won't work? Besides, genies are far more powerful than we think! You know the Forbidden Wishes? They're not forbidden at all, they just need the right circumstances! I've managed to kill this night because I was in great danger! And believe me; we'll all be in great danger if we get there! You can do anything if you think you can! Just believe you can do it! Now who's with me?!' Chris raised his hand and it began to glow with white light.

In the crowd, Joe did the same. Miss Sato followed suit. Miss Torment raised hers and barked: 'Come on punks! Into the fray!'

Sure enough, many of Chris' classmates raised their glowing hands and gradually the entire crowd was filled with glowing hands raised in the air. Soon there wasn't a single genie whose hand wasn't raised and shining brightly.

Chris smiled at them all, and then shouted: 'For Mr Djinn!' The genies cheered.

'For Genie Academy!' There was another cheer.

'For the magical world!' A third cheer sounded.

'For Lucy.' Chris added under his breath.

Then he cried: 'One! Two!! THREE!!!'

A blinding flash enveloped the whole of the academy of genies in white light, and then disappeared, taking them all with it.

Lucy and the archaeologists were standing beside the stone circle just a few moments after Chris left. She had no idea where she and the other captives were going to run to, she was hoping Chris and the genies would get there before they were caught. But just as they prepared to set out, Yvonne's entire banshee force swooped down from above, forming a moving, snarling ring around the stone circle. They were surrounded. One of the banshees stepped out, facing Lucy and the others. 'Come with usssss.' it hissed at them.

'What for? What are you going to do to us?' demanded Lucy, glaring at the speaker. The lead banshee turned to one of its comrades. 'Get herrrr.' it ordered. With a snarl, the underling flew at Lucy.

But before it reached her it was shot down with a red bolt of lightning. Lucy, the other captives and the bewildered banshees looked up. It had come from Chris, who was standing atop one of the stone blocks.

'Did you miss me?' he asked innocently. As one, the banshees rushed at him. 'Oh GENIES!' shouted Chris.

There was a burst of light from the centre of the circle and hundreds of flying genies flew straight out and collided with the banshee swarm. The banshees were driven back amid shouts, snarls and flashes of magic. Chris leapt from his pillar and landed beside Lucy.

'Run!' he shouted before shooting more crimson bolts at the banshees. Lucy did as she was told and led the other people away from the fight. Their path was blocked by banshee reinforcements but then came a cry of: 'Out of the way, punks!' and the attackers were quickly blasted to pieces by Miss Torment and several of Chris' classmates.

An explosion of light came from the other side of the stone circle, and a fiery comet came streaking towards the melee. Mr Djinn, having seen his daughter and his beloved genies in danger, had broken free from his chains at last using a combination of his exploding power and the death spell.

Now he swooped from out of the sky to join the battle.

The whole area was pandemonium now, as genies and banshees fought in the sky and on the ground. The banshees, despite their size and life draining powers, were overwhelmed by sheer numbers and the genies' magic.

Unfortunately, it was this moment that Yvonne chose to join the melee.

She appeared inside the circle holding in her hand the Elf Heart and used it to fire a death spell at a nearby genie. The man was vaporised instantly. Not even immortal beings could withstand the power of the Elf Heart.

Laughing, Yvonne rose into the air and fired it amongst the genies, causing explosions to throw them off their feet and killing any genie that was caught by the blast.

From a distance, Lucy saw what Yvonne was doing. She realised that if the fairy wasn't stopped then she could kill all of them with that weapon. Ignoring the protests of her fellow captives, she ran towards the battle scene, avoiding banshees and explosions of magic. She saw Yvonne standing on the same stone structure that Chris had appeared on, and ran unseen towards her. When she thought she was close enough, she relaxed herself. Another thing Mind Readers can do is use their minds to levitate objects. Lucy hadn't tried it so far, but she knew it would be quite easy once she concentrated.

Yvonne felt the Elf Heart being tugged from her grasp. She tried to hold on, but was unable to keep hold. Eventually it dragged her from the stone and she fell to the ground, dropping the weapon. Lucy quickly picked it up but Yvonne was coming straight for her. Lucy shouted at Chris, who was running to help her, and threw him the Elf Heart. He caught it just as Yvonne reached Lucy. Yvonne struck her with the back of her hand and Lucy was thrown to the ground. The fairy then saw Chris coming towards them, the Elf Heart tucked in his pocket. She summoned a magic shield to enclose the stone circle, trapping all the other genies who were still busy fighting the losing banshees on the other side.

Yvonne blasted lightning at Chris. He deflected the barrage and it destroyed one of the megaliths. Yvonne then levitated two of the other stones off the floor and threw them at Chris. He flew above them and they both smashed into each other. Yvonne threw another at him. He blew it up in midair and the remains fell at his feet. Then both enemies shot a killing spell at each other, and the spells were locked in a globe of light as they struggled for mastery.

Something had to give.

The globe exploded and Chris and Yvonne were blown off their feet. Yvonne rolled to the base of a surviving stone, and as she got up she saw Chris' lamp lying a few feet away. Her hand grasped it, and fire blossomed.

Chris screamed and writhed on the ground as the fairy circled him.

'Where is the Elf Heart?' she hissed. Chris continued to cry as Yvonne circled him. 'I won't finish with you until you're begging for death! And only when you are grovelling at my feet will I put you out of your misery! This is what happens to anyone who interferes with me! And that's how people will remember you! As the boy who always interfered!'

Lucy seized her chance and ran up behind the

demented fairy, pushing her to the ground. The lamp flew out of her hand, and Lucy grabbed it, putting it behind her back. Yvonne got back up and advanced on her.

'I would have spared you.' The fairy said with a mad look in her eyes. 'But you decided to help him instead. And now you will die with him!'

'No she won't.' said Chris.

Yvonne looked back at him and saw he held the Elf Heart in his hand. Before she could stop him a beam of red light shot from the metal sphere and hit her squarely in the chest. The force field over the circle vanished. The fairy fell to the floor, eyes still open, staring unseeing at the night sky.

The surviving banshees took up their famous howl for their fallen leader, and then flew away into the night. With the battle for Stonehenge over, the first rays of sun began to light up the sky. A new day was dawning.

Freedom

The morning after the battle of Stonehenge, Chris and Lucy stood together in Lucy's bedroom. They were both exhausted, especially Chris who had stayed an extra hour helping the genies repair the Stonehenge circle at the insistence of the archaeologists. This was despite Miss Torment's protest that the thing was five thousand years old so it was falling to bits anyway.

'What happened to the Elf Heart?' asked Chris.

'I put it back in the chamber. It's caused enough trouble,' answered Lucy

Chris nodded.

'What will you do now?' he asked.

'Dad said we should bury Yvonne first,' answered Lucy.

'And then?'

'Don't know.'

'Well, you can leave that to me,' said Mr Djinn, entering the room. 'Given that you need someone to look after you, and since I am your father, I feel it's my duty to take care of you from now on. Though how I'm going to explain my being missing presumed dead for thirteen years I really don't know.'

'Great!' said Chris. 'But who will run the Genie

Academy sir?'

'Well, I don't think I'm quite ready to step down just yet. But since Lucy now possesses my ring, I should be able to run the Genie Academy *and* live in the mortal world. Visiting the place during her school hours should be fine!'

'So what happens to me?' asked Chris.

'Well,' said Lucy. 'You still haven't granted me my third wish yet.'

'Oh no! I haven't! What'll it be, then? A pony? Nah, you're too old for that sort of thing. Maybe your very own yacht. Actually no, the Thames isn't a good place for sailing a yacht. How about a dog? That's a bit simple actually, how about a talking dog? Someone you can have conversations with and play fetch with! Now that's quality!'

'I wish for your freedom.' said Lucy.

Chris stared at her.

'What? Really? Say that again!'

'Have a look at your lamp,' said Mr Djinn.

Chris did as he said and noticed his lamp sitting on the cupboard beside Lucy's bed. It was glowing. Chris lit up from inside and a stream of golden light flowed from him into the lamp's spout, taking all his magic with it. When the process was over, a symbol in the shape of a spiral appeared on the side.

Chris picked it up and examined it in bewilderment.

'What just happened?' he asked both Lucy and Mr Djinn.

'You're free,' said Mr Djinn. 'All your magic is now inside that lamp. You can tell it's a genie's lamp by the symbol. Of course if you want to use it you'll have to rub the lamp and get your magic back; but you're now a free man... boy... genie... whatever.'

'So I'm just a normal person now.' said Chris, just as overwhelmed as he was on his first day at Genie Academy.

'Normal as you'll ever be.' said Lucy.

'Is that a compliment or an insult?'

'And you should get your memory back,' Mr Djinn pointed out.

'Really? Oh, I see what you mean. Blimey, I have a house in Cheshire. And a family. A mum and dad, and a sister. Oh, big sister. I've got a dog. And what's the date?'

'The third of February,' answered Lucy.

'But it was early January when I first met Yvonne! I've been missing a whole month! My parents are going to be furious! I ought to get home. Actually, how am I going to get there? Train? I'm going to need money!'

'We can lend you some,' offered Lucy.

'Really? Thanks. Oh boy, there's going to be fireworks.'

'Well, as fun as that sounds, I ought to go and call my lawyer,' said Mr Djinn. 'He'll certainly get a shock hearing my voice after all these years.' He shook Chris by the hand. 'Look after yourself old fellow. And don't use that lamp unless you have to, understand? You've seen what trouble magic can cause. And good luck in the mortal world.'

'Thanks. For everything.'

Mr Djinn nodded. 'Be back in a tick Lucy.' And with a quick salute he exited the room.

Chris turned to Lucy. 'Well, what can I say?' he said. 'Thank you.'

'What for? I was only repaying you for all you've done. You saved my life. In more ways than one,' replied Lucy.

Chris grinned. 'Suppose I did. Do you think we could keep in touch and visit each other once in a while?'

'I'd like that.'

'Great. Er, here.' Chris took out a slip of paper and a pen. He wrote something down and then handed it to Lucy. 'You ever need me, here's the number to call.' he said as she took it.

'Thanks. And next time you see me, I hope you've improved on your cooking skills,' said Lucy.

Chris laughed. 'Me too. No more chocolate milkshakes until I have.'

'Good. I'll see you round then, Chris Forrester.'

'Yeah. You'll be alright without your all-powerful slave, won't you?'

'I've got my all-powerful dad looking after me.'

'True. Goodbye then. And thanks again.' Then they hugged, and when they'd separated Chris picked up his lamp and put it in a safe pocket.

'Hope I won't need this for a while,' he said with a smile.

'Indeed. But when your phone rings and I'm on the other end, you'd better come running with that close to hand,' said Lucy.

'I'm waiting with bated breath.'

And with that Chris left with his lamp, and Lucy was alone again. She might have lost Yvonne, but she'd found her real father and a funny new friend.

A few hours later, Mr Djinn visited the Genie Academy to make sure everything was alright. The genies killed in the battle of Stonehenge were being given a special genie burial. The ones whose bodies survived were put in floating glass coffins and sent off into the horizon over the expanse of cloud. Those whose bodies were destroyed had memorial tablets embedded in the walls of the academy. When the funeral was over, Mr Djinn met Joe standing watching the coffins fly away into the distance.

'What happened to Chris?' asked Joe.

'Free,' answered Mr Djinn. 'Though I don't think it's the last we'll see of him. I expect when he's found his family and sorted out whatever mess he left behind, he'll start looking for ways to set the rest of us free.'

'You sure about that?'

'Would you ever doubt him?'

Joe shook his head.

'Of course not. It's just... sometimes I wonder if I really want to be freed. I wonder if I really want to find out who the girl in my locket is, and why I have such horrible nightmares.'

'We all have nightmares sometimes, Joe.'

'None as vivid as mine. Chris and Lucy got a happy ending, but what happens to the rest of us in the end? Do you think anyone cares if we get our happy ending?'

Mr Djinn put an arm around Joe's shoulders. 'Someday Joe, we will all get our happy ending.'

Chris turned into his street. He recognised everything, from the houses lining each side to the trees on each corner. Even birds in the trees seemed familiar, and the song brought back floods of memories. At last he saw the home he knew as his own, sitting cosily between two other houses.

As he walked slightly apprehensively towards the doorstep he realised he had no idea what he would say to the person who opened that door, how he would explain where he had been and what he had done. But then again, home was worth the trouble.

Besides; he had unfinished business. Loki was still missing; last seen disappearing in a colourful explosion. Yvonne said she had sent him somewhere no-one would find him, but Chris intended to do so no matter what the cost.

But first he had to see to his family. As he rang the doorbell, Chris Forrester realised that one adventure might be over, but another was just beginning.